Jennifer crossed the hall to the parlor, still angry that her father had asked her to apologize to Mr. Meares. She found writing paper and pen and sat down to write.

In what was supposed to be a note of apology, it would scarcely have been appropriate to describe the fury which still arose within her as she recalled the cutting words he had spoken to her before storming out of her house.

But she could vividly remember the physical reaction he had roused in her, pleasurable and exciting. The memory troubled her, because her body had betrayed her into feeling attracted toward a man whose character appeared to be in direct contrast to the values she most admired and respected in the opposite sex.

Landscape
of the Heart

ELIZABETH RENIER

FAWCETT CREST • NEW YORK

LANDSCAPE OF THE HEART

THIS BOOK CONTAINS THE COMPLETE TEXT OF
THE ORIGINAL HARDCOVER EDITION.

Published by Fawcett Crest Books, a unit of CBS Publications, the Consumer Publishing Division of CBS Inc., by arrangement with the Hutchinson Publishing Group.

ISBN: 0-449-23970-5

Printed in the United States of America

10 9 8 7 6 5 4 3 2 1

For Robert and Jill, the present owners of the house I have called "Heronslea"

Chapter One

As the four horses strained to pull the heavy wagon up the steep, winding hill which led to Moreton-hampstead, Jennifer Haslam peered eagerly through a gap in the canvas cover. Her spirits rose as she caught sight of the lights of the little moorland town shining through the September twilight, and happy anticipation banished the weariness of the long journey from London. The speed of the train which had carried her from Paddington to Exeter had been exhilarating, but for the last four hours she had been jolted and thrown about in this cumbersome vehicle euphemistically described as a horse-omnibus. Within minutes now she would be set down at the White Hart Inn where Alan Vicary would be waiting to take her the last few miles to Lidbridge and home. After nearly two years' exile—for that was how Jennifer thought of her stay in London—she would be back on her beloved Dartmoor, reunited with her father and free to mix with people she understood and with whom she could talk about things that really mattered instead of making polite and trivial conversation with Londoners who had seemed almost foreigners to her, so different were their interests and attitudes.

Yet Aunt Lucy's invitation had been well-intentioned.

It will be the making of Jennifer, she had written to her brother, Professor Haslam, two years ago when Jennifer had been seventeen. *She is such a lively, charming girl and much too intelligent to be buried in that dreary wilderness where you choose to live. I shall enjoy her company and shall doubtless be able to arrange a suitable marriage. If she remains under your roof she will probably end up as wife to one of those dreadful yokels whose speech I found impossible to comprehend.*

To Jennifer's surprise, her father had agreed. "It will give you the opportunity to find out whether the fuller life of the city appeals to you," he had said, "and it is right that you should widen your horizons."

She had not wanted to go, and she had been concerned as to how he would manage. Since her mother's death she had not only looked after his physical well-being but also helped him in his work. He had assured her he would manage well enough with the widow Westcott acting as housekeeper and although he would miss her assistance in his work he was determined not to be selfish and let her miss this chance offered by his sister.

Clement Haslam, a product of Oxford University, had originally visited Dartmoor to study the antiques. A satchel on his back, compass and map in his pocket, he had diligently sought out every cromlech and menhir, every stone row and group of hut circles on the moor. At night, in the little parlour of Lidden Barton, he had set down his findings and his theories as to the origins of these prehistoric remains. For years now he had been regarded as an expert, his opinions sought by learned gentlemen in all parts of the civilized world, his books receiving high praise.

Jennifer had often wondered how such a seemingly ill-assorted pair as her parents had come to marry. Her father had been a middle-aged scholar, absent-minded, his thoughts centred mostly on the past. Her mother came of hardy farming stock and was plump, pretty, full of vitality and laughter.

It was just before she died that she answered Jennifer's unspoken question.

"I married your father because he needed looking after and because he treated me as if I were the grandest lady in the land. I've never understood his work but that's not mattered. I've kept his house and mended his clothes and seen that he ate properly. I've kept him happy, Jenny, and that's what a woman's born for, I reckon, to keep a man happy and bear her children, but there's some that have other ideas, I know."

In London Jennifer had met with those other ideas and in several women she had sensed, beneath the surface smoothness of their marriages, an undercurrent of boredom and antagonism. She had therefore taken a good hard look at each of the young men Aunt Lucy had produced as possible suitors and not one of them, in her estimation, matched up to Alan Vicary, her childhood friend and the sweetheart of her adolescent years. It would have been different, of course, if she had been swept off her feet, fallen headlong in love as the other young women seemed prone to do quite easily and she was really quite relieved that it had not happened when she saw how foolishly it made them behave.

Alan was twenty-one now, the only son of a moorland farmer. His own heart was in farming, too, but unlike his father, who was content to continue in the old ways, Alan was progressively minded. He had been one of several children taught elementary lessons by her father and it had been Professor Haslam who had persuaded Alan's mother that he should be sent to a grammar school. Not that she had needed much persuading, for she was ambitious for her son.

School had worked wonders for Alan. At home he still used the local dialect but in public he could converse freely with any man, his Devonshire accent no different from that used by most people in the county in the mid-nineteenth century. He had recognized at once the subjects which would prove most useful to him, and, his easy-going nature being off-set by a stubborn streak, had steadfastly refused to waste his time studying those which would not be of benefit. He was single-minded in his ambition to have a farm of his own which he could build up into the biggest and most modern on the moor. He knew that the odds against him were great, that it would be a long time before he could attain that end, for his parents had two daughters to provide for besides themselves and life on one of the ancient tenements of Dartmoor was a perpetual struggle against poor soil, a hard climate and lack of capital.

Jennifer had been longing to see him, but as the wagon lumbered into Moretonhampstead, she wondered what he would think of her, dressed as she was in a smart travelling costume of green bombasine with a matching cloak and poke bonnet. She wore black mittens and carried a reticule and her dark hair was dressed in the smooth, plain style made popular by the young Queen Victoria. She was still as slim as she had been when she left home and it had been too much to hope that she would have added any more inches to her height. The queen was also a very small lady, Aunt Lucy had told her niece when she had come upon Jennifer scowling into a mirror when trying on a new ball gown.

She had attended a great number of balls, and supper parties and concerts. She had spent many afternoons going for carriage drives when she would have much preferred to be riding, but Aunt Lucy considered horse-riding a most unfeminine recreation. She also disapproved of young girls walking any distance, although it was Jennifer's private opinion that in carrying out all the trivial errands which seemed of so much importance to her aunt, she must have walked nearly as many miles in one morning as she had previously done tramping across the moor.

But all that was over now, and as the wagon turned into the yard of the inn, she saw Alan. He was standing beneath a wall lamp, the light burnishing his dark auburn hair, for, as usual, he was bareheaded. He was wearing a new suit of brown broadcloth and his brown boots were shining with polish. Jennifer was so used by now to the company of men dressed almost uniformly in frock-coats and black top hats that Alan's appearance came as a shock to her, and he seemed bigger than she remembered, his shoulders broader, his body sturdier. For a moment he seemed almost a stranger and she had an odd feeling of panic.

Then, as the wagon drew up and Alan stepped forward, her sense of shock was banished by a glow of warmth as she saw his arms upstretched in welcome, the pleasure shining in his hazel eyes. The next moment she was lifted down as if she weighed no more than thistledown.

"Jenny," he said softly, "it's been so long. Let me

look at you." He held her at arms' length, his gaze taking every detail. "My, but you're a grand lady now!"

She laughed up at him. "It's the clothes. *I'm* not any different."

"Is that true?"

She heard the note of doubt in his voice and said quickly, "Of course it's true. Town life isn't for me. I felt shut in and I hated the smells and the noise and never being alone and quiet. People in London seem to have to keep talking all the time."

"What about?"

"The men talk about politics and money. Girls chatter endlessly about beaux and clothes and the older women complain about servants or the price of butter. I doubt if more than a handful of them know that butter comes originally from a cow. And Aunt Lucy is for ever fussing about trivialities and I doubt that in almost two years I performed a single task that was of the least importance. But I shouldn't be speaking like this. Aunt Lucy meant well and she can't help being ignorant, poor thing. I discovered that except for a few privileged ones, women aren't expected to have much intelligence."

Alan chuckled. "I dare say you gave them a few shocks."

"I'm sure I did," she agreed gaily. "I think Aunt Lucy had led her friends to expect a country bumpkin, so I took great delight in quoting Homer or giving a dissertation on archaeology. And then Aunt

Lucy would hold up her hands and exclaim, 'The nonsense your dear father has stuffed your head with! I'm sure I shall never find a husband for you if you talk like that.' How *is* Papa? I am so longing to see him."

"He was well when I saw him a few days ago but I believe he has grown even more absent-minded and Mrs Westcott has not your mother's patience—or yours. I think she has threatened to leave several times but your father just looks at her over his spectacles and says 'Yes, yes, I should do that, a very good idea.' "

Jennifer burst out laughing and thought how Aunt Lucy would disapprove, both of the unrestrained laughter and of her niece standing in an inn yard talking, unchaperoned, to a young man, and one whom she would doubtless include in her sweeping condemnation of "dreadful yokels".

"You must be very tired after such a long journey," Alan said. "I'll collect your luggage and then we'd best be on our way. Unless you'd like something to eat before we start?"

"I'd rather wait until I get home." She glanced across the yard. "Is that *your* trap?"

Ruefully he shook his head. "I borrowed Mr Venner's." He smiled a little uncertainly. "After all, I could scarcely expect a smart young lady from London to travel home in a farmcart."

"I should have been happy to travel by any

means, even riding pillion with you, so long as it is homewards."

"You hated London so much?" he asked in surprise. "Your letters made it sound . . ."

"No, I didn't hate it. There were many things I enjoyed. It would have been most unnatural at my age not to have done so. But—oh, it's difficult to explain but I felt under pressure most of the time."

"What sort of pressure?" he asked, reaching for her luggage. "Not to do any work, I gather, from what you said just now."

"No. That I should have welcomed. But to behave differently. I was expected to conform, to speak and walk and even think in a prescribed pattern, and always, of course . . ."

"Yes?" he prompted as she broke off.

She did not want to say to Alan, "Always I was under pressure to get married," so she quickly changed the subject and asked after his family.

"Father's rheumatism has been bad lately," he said, transferring her luggage to the trap, "but my sisters have grown into fine strong girls and are a great help."

"And your mother?" she added, a little reluctantly.

He shrugged. "She doesn't alter. You know mother."

She had always found Mrs Vicary difficult to understand, but one thing about her was patently obvious—her devotion to her only son.

"Are you still her 'blue-eyed boy'?" Jennifer asked teasingly.

She expected him to take her teasing as lightly as he had done in the past. Instead, he said shortly, "I'm not a boy now, Jenny. Even if Mother still thinks of me in that way, I don't expect *you* to do so."

"I'm sorry," she said at once, and in that moment she knew why the first sight of him had given her that sense of shock, the feeling that he was almost a stranger. It was not only that he looked so different from the young men with whom she had associated during the past two years, and that he seemed to have grown bigger. In her thoughts she had remembered him as the boy she had known since childhood. Now she saw him as a man, and, moreover, a man born on the granite, strong, self-sufficient, dependable.

As he handed her up into the trap, she said, "Tell me about your sheep. You said they were doing well, on the rare occasions when you wrote."

He took his place beside her and clicked his tongue to the pony. "I'm not much of a hand at letter-writing, as you know. Yes, the sheep have done well, thanks to the dry summer." He went on to tell her, as they left the lights of the town behind, that there had been few losses amongst the lambs, that a pair of dippers had nested as usual beneath the packhorse bridge, that the fishing had been poor because of the lack of water in the rivers, that his collie bitch had produced a fine litter of pups and he had sold them well for they came of a line of notable sheep-dogs.

"I would have saved one for you," he added, "if I hadn't known that your father isn't partial to dogs."

"That's always been a sore point with me, as it was with Mama. We must be about the one house on the moor without a dog."

"At least you'll not be without a pony to ride."

"What do you mean? Surely Papa has not thought to . . . ?"

"No, not your father. You remember my filly foal with the white blaze on her nose that you took such a fancy to? I broke her in for you, then borrowed your side-saddle and put Alice up on her a time or two."

"Oh, Alan, that *is* good of you! And so generous, too, for she would have fetched a fair price at the October sales, wouldn't she?"

"I dare say," he said gruffly because he was embarrassed. "But you wrote that you longed to ride again, and so . . ."

"It's not only the mare herself but the time you must have spent." She slipped her arm through his. "When I thought about you in London, as I often did, one of the things I remembered most was your kindness. I brought you back a present, I hope you'll like it."

"Of course I shall, but the only present I really want is . . . Well, time enough for that."

She was glad he had gone no further. There was so much time ahead and no need for quick decisions or commitments. It was going to be simple to slip back into their former easy relationship. She rested her head against his shoulder as he let the pony take its time on the long climb up to the moor. Now they were alone under the stars, with the great sweep of open country on either side. There were no houses here, nothing but a group of wild ponies, dark shapes against the skyline, and the pale running forms of sheep, startled by the lanterns' light and the sound of wheels. She breathed deeply of the moorland air which smelled of peat and bracken and the last of the heather. She was growing sleepy now. Her head fell forward and Alan put his arm about her to support her.

The road was running downhill. Then they reached level ground and passed some cottages, the dissenting chapel, the inn. To Jennifer's surprise she noticed what looked like lighted windows away to their right. There was no dwelling-place there, only the ruins of Heronslea, a gothic-style house with turrets and narrow windows, begun at the turn of the century and abandoned because of lack of money. It had long been the haunt of owls and other wild creatures, visited by only the most venturesome of the local children. Jennifer was puzzled by the lights and thought of questioning Alan about them, but it seemed too much effort, and then she forgot about them as he took a sharp turn left into the lane which led to Lidden Barton.

She sat up straight now, alert with anticipation. As they reached the open space in front of the house the door was flung open and the solid figure of Mrs Westcott was silhouetted against the lamplight. The housekeeper hurried forward as Jennifer stepped down.

"Thank the Lord you be safe, Miss Jenny! I've been that worrited about you, coming all that way on your lonesome. I kept thinking of all the dreadful things that could have happened to you. Come into the warm, you must be fair schrammed."

"Where is Papa?" asked Jennifer in surprise as she entered the house.

"I'm to give you a message," Mrs Westcott said, looking embarrassed.

"A *message?* You mean that Papa is not here?"

"He've gone to Plymouth, Miss Jenny."

"Surely he knew I was coming home today?"

"Yes, but . . . You know how forgetful he is. There was a meeting of some society . . ."

"The Plymouth Institution?"

"That'll be it. He was to read a paper, seemingly, something to do with they old stones he'm so fond of. He'd forgotten about it until the Reverend Mr Taverner called for him in his carriage. Your father was very upset but he said you'd understand he had to go, to fulfil his obligation, was how he did put it."

Jennifer felt as if someone had thrown a pail of

cold river water over her. She had looked forward so eagerly to this moment, knowing her father would not be demonstrative but picturing his welcoming smile, the unnecessary polishing of his spectacles which meant he was deeply moved. She would not see him now until tomorrow. He and the parson always stayed with friends in Plymouth after a meeting, to avoid the long drive back over the moor in the dark.

Alan had brought in her luggage. "Never mind," he said cheerfully. "It will be something still to look forward to."

"Yes, you're right," she said, smiling at him gratefully because his words had helped her through this moment of anticlimax. "Will you have something to eat before you . . . ?"

"No, thanks. I'd best be getting along. I promised Mr Venner to return the trap tonight. He has to be in court tomorrow."

"In court?"

"He's a magistrate now. Didn't you know?"

She shook her head. "I suppose a number of things have happened that I don't know about. People told me so little in their letters. Papa, of course, wrote . . ."

"Now come along, Miss Jenny," the housekeeper urged. "Into the parlour with you and have a warmup while I fetch you something to eat. You look proper peaky and I'm not surprised after all that travelling. I'll just take this small valise up to your room and the bigger luggage can wait until morning when Zebedee . . ."

"Zebedee?"

"He'm the new boy for outside work and looking after that grand little mare Alan's give you. Zebedee's a willing enough worker but a bit wanting up top, poor lad."

"Would you like me to carry up the luggage?" Alan offered.

Mrs Westcott flung up her hands in horror. "Go up to Miss Jennifer's bedroom? I never heard the like! I'm sure it was very good of you to fetch her from Moreton but, as you said, 'tis time you were on your way."

As the housekeeper disappeared up the stairs, Jennifer chuckled. "Mrs Westcott certainly hasn't changed."

"I can't believe *you* haven't, Jenny. After all, nearly two years of . . ."

"I haven't changed, Alan, believe me!" she declared earnestly. "Not in any important way, I mean."

"I hope not," he said, doubt still in his voice. "You see, I—I'm finding it difficult to believe you're really back. Sometimes, when I got your letters, I was almost afraid to open them in case . . . well, Mother kept saying you'd be sure to fall in love and marry some fine young gentleman . . ."

"Your mother was wrong," she said, more sharply than she intended. "I didn't fall in love, though

goodness knows I had chance enough. And I *am*
back, and I'm here to stay and I never want to
leave the moor again."

His face lit up. He bent and gave her a quick,
light kiss on her cheek. Then he was gone, calling a
husky good night as he went out into the chill September darkness.

In the parlour Jennifer took off her bonnet and
cloak. The thought came to her of how shocked
Aunt Lucy would have been had she observed that
kiss, harmless and almost brotherly as it had been.
In her aunt's book of rules a young man did not
kiss a young lady until they were betrothed and
even then not without asking permission. But she
was home now and Aunt Lucy's rules no longer
held sway.

Contentedly she looked round the room. The
shutters were drawn and in the soft light of fire and
lamps everything was just as she remembered, every
piece of furniture, every ornament in exactly the
same place. Above the granite hearthstone hung a
portrait of her mother, alongside it one of herself
as a child. They had been painted by a young artist
who had been staying at the Duchy Hotel in Princetown. He had come upon Mary Haslam, dressed in
printed muslin and a sun-bonnet, working in the
garden and asked if he might paint her. She had
given him home-made bread and butter and clotted
cream and strawberry jam. Then, treating the affair
as a joke, she had sat for him. He had painted her in

the romantic style so fashionable at the time, against a background of heather and gorse, a kitten playing at her feet. Afterwards, she had asked if he would paint Jennifer too, and he had done a water-colour impression of a child standing on the foot-bridge over the river. Then he had signed both paintings and presented them to her mother. Jennifer had often wondered if the young artist had made a success of his work and while in London she had made enquiries but no one she had asked had ever heard of him.

Mrs Westcott came in with a tray. Jennifer suddenly felt so weary that food held little attraction for her but she dutifully drank the soup and ate a little bread and butter, thankful that the housekeeper did not remain to talk or ask questions. Twenty minutes later she was snuggled into the soft folds of her feather mattress, listening to the sounds familiar since babyhood—the river purling and foaming around moss-covered boulders, the hooting of a tawny owl in the beech trees above the stable, the whisper of leaves stirred by the night breeze. Above the dark mass of the encircling hills the sky was bright with stars. Nothing had changed. Tomorrow she could take up her old life again as if she had never been away. The peace of the little valley closed about her, as dear and reassuring as her mother's arms had been in childhood. Sighing with happiness, she drifted into sleep.

Jennifer's first sight of Zebedee was when she went to look at the mare Alan had given her. Mrs Westcott had insisted on taking her up a breakfast tray, telling her that she might as well have a lie-in as there was such a thick mist. "You'd scare see a crow if he perched on your nose". When Jennifer had learned that Ada, their maid-of-all-work, had been allowed home because her mother was ill, she had offered to help in the house, but Mrs Westcott had laid down the law over that, too.

"There be a pile of work waiting for you in the study and I reckon your father'll have you hard at it so soon as he gets back. But that'll not be until tea-time at least, for that old coachman of Mr Taverner's won't venture on the moor in this weather. Scared of mist, he is, ever since he got lost down to Fox Tor Mire as a lad. So you may as well have a good rest while you can."

Jennifer had stayed in bed for a while, reading the notes of welcome and some invitations which had awaited her return. Then, as the mist seemed to be clearing a little, she got up and put on the blue riding habit she had not had any opportunity to wear in London, and made for the stable.

A lad was crossing the yard, carrying hay on a pitchfork. He was short, though solidly built, with a mop of fair hair above a moon face. His lower lip drooped and when he answered her greeting it was in a thick voice, difficult to understand.

"You are Zebedee?" Jennifer asked.

He nodded eagerly. " 'Ees, that I be. You be Miss Jennifer what I've yeard about? Come all the way from Lunnon on one of they gurt iron monsters?"

"By train? Yes, that's right."

His gaze went over her in childlike curiosity. "You'm little, bain't 'ee? I'd not thought you'd be so small. You'll fit the little mare a fair treat."

"You have the care of her, I believe."

Again he nodded vigorously. "That I have, and right good care of her I do take. Mr Vicary, he said he'd skin me alive if I didn't." He grinned, showing gaps in his teeth. "I'm not afeared of he, though. He'd not hurt poor Zebedee." The grin vanished and the boy glanced nervously over his shoulder. "There be some folks I'm afeared of, though. Mrs Westcott when she do get proper testy, and that old witch that do live up by Gibbet Tor, and the big black man . . ."

"What big black man?" Jennifer asked as she went into the stable.

"Him that do open the door up to Heronslea. A giant 'ee be, I do swear."

Recalling that Mrs Westcott had said the lad was "a bit wanting up top," Jennifer said casually, "You're imagining things, Zebedee. There's no black man . . ."

"That there be, then," he declared obstinately. "I've seen un and I'm more afeared of he than I am of Drewer and his wish hounds."

I'm certainly back on Dartmoor, Jennifer thought

with tolerant amusement, what with witches and the devil and a phantom black man who opens doors at a ruined house. Then she remembered the lights she had noticed as Alan drove her through Lidbridge, and she wondered if someone was playing a joke up at Heronslea, frightening poor witless souls like Zebedee. The next moment she forgot the whole affair, she was so delighted by the sight of the little mare.

She spent a while making friends with the pony, then instructed the lad to saddle and bridle the mare while she went to tell Mrs Westcott that despite the mist she was determined on a ride, even if it was no further than along the rough meadows beside the river.

The housekeeper fully approved. "You do still look peaky. A ride'll put some roses back in your cheeks. If the mist should clear and you do want to go and see your friends and stay for a bite of dinner, you do that, I know Mollie Perrott's been counting the days until your return, wanting to show off her baby. I don't hold with christenings being delayed but she was that determined on you being godmother."

Jennifer went upstairs to fetch her gloves and hat. On the way out, she glanced into her father's study. It was in its usual state of disarray but she knew better than to attempt to tidy it. Neither she nor her mother had ever been allowed in the study unless her father was present. She had come to accept the untidiness as being as much part of her father as his absent-mindedness.

When she rode out of the yard, moisture was dripping from the trees in an uneven pattern of sound. A wren stuttered its alarm from a gorse bush and a robin's thin autumn song came from the holly tree. A heron flew up the valley and she greeted it like an old friend. As long as she could remember there had been a heron on this stretch of the river, although the heronry which had given Heronslea its name had long since been deserted, after a gale had destroyed some of the trees.

The mist was still thick to the north but it was clearing downstream, the direction in which she wanted to go. Gorse blossom glowed brightly through the greyness and the river was milky white where it tumbled over mossy rocks. As Jennifer rounded a bend in the river she came into sunshine. She urged the little mare into a canter and the animal responded at once, seeming to take as much pleasure in her new owner as Jennifer had done at sight of Alan's gift.

Hearing the mewing of a buzzard, Jennifer reined in to watch the bird as it soared high overhead. Then, following its flight, she saw a horseman silhouetted on the skyline. His mount was not a moorland pony like hers but a handsome chestnut thoroughbred with flowing mane and tail, and it was causing its rider a great deal of trouble.

After watching the battle of wills for a few minutes, Jennifer continued along the valley bottom. Suddenly she realized why the chestnut was refusing so stubbornly to take the path towards which the horseman was urging it. There were standing stones nearby which, according to her father, were part of a pagan sacrificial rite. Whatever their origin, it was well known that some horses and dogs would not go near them. If a horse was forced to do so, it sweated and showed every sign of terror.

Jennifer turned her mare towards the hill, intending to warn the horseman. Before she had a chance to do so, the chestnut reared, then plunged violently, unseating its rider. The man tried to hold on to the reins but the terrified animal was too strong for him and bolted.

Jennifer knew she had no chance of catching it. In any case, her first concern was for the rider. But it looked as if he was unhurt, for he was already on his feet and shaking his fist at the retreating chestnut. He was a very tall man, she saw, and caught a glimpse of fair hair before he replaced his beaver hat. He wore a bottle-green coat and light breeches. Such a well-dressed stranger, riding alone on a splendid thoroughbred, was probably staying at a hotel in Princetown, which meant he would have a long walk. Jennifer felt some satisfaction at that thought. It had been his own fault that he had been thrown. If a man did not know the difference between an obstinate horse and a frightened horse he had no business to be riding at all.

She used just those words to her friend Mollie Perrott when a little while later she was sitting in Mollie's small cottage adjoining the smithy at Wellsworthy. Mollie had been brought up in the lonely warren house set amidst the artificial rabbit burrows extending over many acres above the ruins of Heronslea. Like Alan, she had been accepted as a pupil in her early years by Professor Haslam. Just before Jennifer left for London, Mollie had married Tom Perrott, blacksmith and farrier. She was short, plump and habitually cheerful, and now, Jennifer saw, there was a new radiance about her and it was with great pride that she had put her six-month-old son into his godmother's arms.

It was when the baby had settled back to sleep that Jennifer mentioned the rider who had taken a toss up on the hill near the standing stones.

"Did you say it was a chestnut horse?" Mollie asked.

"Yes, a beautiful creature. I do hope that stupid man doesn't punish it."

"I should think he's very likely to do so," Mollie remarked with uncharacteristic sharpness.

"Do you know who he is then?"

"I do, indeed. He's been here this morning, to have the chestnut shod. I wish it had thrown him so heavily he'd broken his neck."

"Mollie!" Jennifer looked at her friend incredulously. "I've never heard you speak like that before. You sound as if you hated this man."

"So I do, and so do many others around here."

"But why? Who is he, and what has he done?"

"That," said Mollie dramatically, "was Mr Darrell Meares!"

She waited for Jennifer's response and was obviously disappointed when the younger girl looked blank.

"The name doesn't convey anything to me," Jennifer told her. "Remember, I've been away for . . ."

"You *must* know about him. Everybody does. Oh, come on, Jenny, you're not usually slow to . . ."

"I'm not being slow," Jennifer said indignantly. "I just don't . . ."

"You really don't know? But surely someone must have written you . . ."

"You have no idea how little I *was* told in the letters I received in London. Papa, as you would expect, wrote long dissertations about his latest theories. Mrs Westcott simply reported small domestic matters. Alan wrote about the farm and *your* letters were full of Tom and your baby. Not that I blame you, of course," she added hastily, seeing Mollie's frown, "but as to any real news, I was left pretty well in the dark. So now you can have the pleasure of enlightening me."

"It's not what I'd call a pleasure. Mr Meares is an American, from South Carolina, and he's completely demolished the ruins of Heronslea and in their place . . . But you *must* have seen, Jenny, from the hill as you rode over. The new house stands out for miles around."

"There was a mist. But . . . Let me think a minute."

Those lights she had seen had been significant, after all. And that extraordinary remark of Zebedee's about a black man who opened the door "up to Heronslea"?

"Go on, Mollie," she urged. "Tell me all about it."

Her friend settled back in her chair, obviously relishing the idea of imparting news despite what she had said. "Mr Meares is very rich and he's built himself a splendid mansion . . ."

"Up here on the moor? I should have thought he'd find it much too cold, after Carolina. It's a hot place, I believe, and lots of cotton is grown there. He's not going to try that here, I hope," she added, laughing.

"Something almost as stupid—flax and hemp, besides the thousands of trees he's planting."

"Thousands of trees? You must be exaggerating wildly; Heronslea has only a few acres of land."

"That's all changed. This foreigner obtained a lease from the Duchy of Cornwall and he's enclosed an enormous amount of moorland. Jenny, are you sure you've not been told?"

"Of course I'm sure. You don't suppose I could forget anything as sensational as this, do you?"

Mollie took the sleeping baby from Jennifer and

put him in his cradle. When she sat down again her face showed none of its usual cheerfulness. Jennifer listened in growing astonishment and dismay as her friend told her of the changes which had been taking place during her absence, and of which she had been kept in total ignorance.

"That's monstrous!" she exclaimed when Mollie paused for breath. "For the Duchy to allow so much land to be taken from the commoners is downright wicked."

"You know what they're like. One minute they tell us nothing will interfere with our rights of pasturage and turbary and the next they've swung over to the daft ideas of the 'improvers'. This American is rich, don't forget, and the rich always get their way."

"Yes, I saw that in London. The life of the poor there is dreadful beyond anything I ever imagined. Tell me, how has this enclosure affected your father?"

"At least a quarter of the warren has been taken away. That means not only has father less to live on but it's less work for the people downalong who earn money from skin-packing. Rabbit skins are quite valuable nowadays. Father tried to hold out against the enclosure but he has no legal document."

"Your family have been warreners at Lidhead for generations," Jennifer said indignantly.

"D'you think that makes any difference to a man

like Darrell Meares? *His* family, so I'm told, have been slave-owners for generations. You can't imagine that the rights of a few men who find it hard enough anyway to make a living from the moor area are of any importance to a *gentleman* used to treating all but his own kind as having *no* rights?"

Jennifer sat silent and thoughtful while Mollie made tea and cut her a slice of seed cake. Then she asked, "Do you know what Papa's attitude is to this affair?"

Mollie pulled a face as she handed Jennifer her cup. "You know your father, Jenny. He doesn't really live in the world of today. If any of his beloved stones were threatened, I dare say he'd be up in arms soon enough."

"What about Alan? Surely he . . . ?"

"The Vicary's aren't affected. They don't pasture cattle on the east quarter and their peat ties are further south, as you know."

"Have you talked to this Mr Meares about the . . . ?"

"Jenny, I'm only a blacksmith's wife. Can't you understand what I'm trying to tell you? Mr Meares isn't like anyone else we've had on the moor. He doesn't mix, not even with the gentry. He doesn't hunt or shoot. About the only time he's seen in public is when he attends church."

"Then why has he come and settled here?"

"You'd better ask him," Mollie said almost belligerently.

Jennifer's eyes gleamed. "Is that a challenge?"

Mollie put down her cup and looked hard at her friend. Then she said in a pleased voice, "So you *are* still the same Jenny. I wondered, you know, and so did Alan . . ."

"Whether London would change me? Yes, so he said last night. But it *hasn't!*"

"All right, there's no need to sound so cross. People *do* change."

"You haven't."

Mollie laughed good-naturedly. "Of course I have. You can't get married and have a baby without changing in several ways. Why does it matter so much?"

Jennifer said hesitantly, "I'm not quite sure, except that all the time I was away I held on to the thought that everything would be exactly the same when I eventually came home. I don't mean I was unhappy," she added hastily, "but I didn't belong in London, nor amongst the kind of people I met through Aunt Lucy."

"You know, Jenny," her friend said thoughtfully, "you don't really belong in any one world, like other people. It's not that simple for you. Sometimes, despite your advantages, I've felt almost sorry for you."

"Sorry for me!" Jennifer repeated incredulously. "But *why?*"

"It's difficult to explain but what I'm trying to say is that it was all right when we were all children but you're not a child now, and when it comes . . ."

"What *are* you trying to say?" Jennifer demanded as Mollie came to a stop.

But Mollie had got out of her depth. "Forget about it. I'm sure everything will turn out well. Anyway," she added, giving Jennifer's shoulder an affectionate squeeze and changing into dialect, " 'tis grand to have 'ee back, m'dear. I've missed you a lot, Jenny, even though I've been so happy with Tom and the baby."

When Jennifer left Wellsworthy and set out for the Vicarys' farm, she was vaguely troubled by Mollie's strange words, which occupied her mind even to the exclusion of the startling news regarding the Hersonslea enclosure. But she had not gone far before she came upon Alan, gathering bracken for the cattles' winter bedding. Bronze and golden, the stalks as brittle and sharp as glass, it was piled high on a two-wheeled cart. Alan was about to throw a retaining rope over the load.

"Wait, I'll help you," Jennifer called, sliding from the saddle.

"How do you like the little mare?" he asked, his pleasure at seeing her showing clearly in his face and voice.

"She's beautiful, so gentle and yet with plenty of spirit. We're friends already. I haven't thought of a name yet. Yes, I have," she corrected herself, "this very minute. I'll call her Bracken."

Alan laughed. "It's as good a name as any. Can you catch the rope if I throw it over?"

"Of course I can." She caught it easily and made it fast.

"That'll do fine," Alan said, coming round to her side of the cart.

Jennifer flung her arms wide. "Oh, it's so wonderful to be back! To breathe moorland air again and have so much space all around me, and not to have to talk endlessly about trivialities. I feel alive again, really alive!" She felt in the pocket of her skirt. "Here's the present I brought for you, Alan. You'd better wash your hands, though."

Alan burst out laughing. "That's one of the first things you ever said to me. I thought you were a bossy little prig."

"I probably still am," she said cheerfully, "Bossy, I mean—when I get the chance."

Still laughing, Alan rinsed his hands in the little stream tinkling along between lichen-covered boulders, then rubbed them dry on his breeches.

"Now cup your hands and close your eyes," Jennifer ordered.

"That's something else I remember," he said, carrying out her instructions. "You were always one for surprises."

As she looked at his hands, strong, tanned by the sun, toughened by hard work, it was her turn to remember, how gentle those hands could be with children and beasts. She put into them the present on which she had expended so much thought, then watched his face as he stared incredulously at the watch in its silver case.

At last he said, in an awed voice, "This must have cost . . ."

"Never mind what it cost. Do you like it?"

He seemed lost for words, then resorted to a typical Devonshire expression. " 'Tis hansome, real handsome. I've never had such a present, not in all my life."

When he had looked his fill, he slid the watch back into its chamois case. "I'll cherish it always," he said. "Keep it for Sundays and special days."

"In that case, don't forget to wind it," she said, laughing. "I don't want to have to spend my time reminding you about things in the same way that I do for Papa."

As she saw the way he was looking at her, and realised the meaning he could have put on her words, the colour flooded into her cheeks. She said quickly, "I dare say your father will call it a waste of money and say that the sun should be good enough for you to tell the time by."

"Oh, Father'd still use rushlight if he had his way. And talking of Father, I'd best be getting back, Jenny. He'll be waiting to spread this load. Were you on your way over to us?"

"Yes. I'll follow you."

Edgecombe Farm was one of the oldest settlements on this part of the moor and had been leased by the Vicary family from the Duchy of Cornwall for generations. The buildings, grouped around the original longhouse, had walls of solid moorstone and roofs of thick reed-thatch. In the yard, chickens scatched vigorously beside the peat stack and a bull bellowed forlornly from the shippon. Alan's father, a man who seemed to regard speech like money, to be used only when the need was essential, gave Jennifer a friendly nod in greeting, just as if she had been away no more than a day. Then his mother came to the back door, wiping her hands on her pinafore.

"Why, 'tis Jenny Haslam. And what a grand lady you'm looking, for sure." She turned to Alan. "Help her down, boy."

Alan, untying the ropes binding the load of bracken, stared at his mother in surprise. "Jenny can get off a pony by herself," he said. "She's done so ever since she was a little girl."

"She's not a little girl now," Mrs Vicary said severely. "You'll do as I say, and hand her down."

Flushing, Alan started across the yard but Jennifer slid from the saddle and tethered Bracken to a ring in the wall. "I don't want to interrupt the work, Mrs Vicary," she said lightly. "I rode over to see you and the girls."

She followed Alan's mother into the kitchen where Bertha, the younger daughter, was putting the finishing touches to an apple pie. The girl looked up with an eager smile, then became suddenly tongue-tied as Jennifer greeted her.

"Sit you down by the fire," Mrs Vicary said, "and I'll bring you a glass of my potato wine. Turned out a fair treat it did, this year."

The copper warming-pan and bellows gleamed in the sunlight slanting through the low window. A huge black kettle hung as always on the hook above the range. The grandfather clock ticked with slow solemnity beside the dresser where blue and white plates were meticulously arranged on the shelves. A cat was curled up asleep on the high-backed oak settle. The whole atmosphere of the farmhouse kitchen was redolent of continuity, a changelessness which should have made for a sense of peace and security. Yet, as always, the presence of Alan's mother made Jennifer feel uneasy. Admittedly, she had been made welcome and offered hospitality but she felt, stronger than ever, the older woman's latent hostility.

Mrs Vicary was a good-looking woman, with dark hair and eyes, high cheek-bones and thick, arched eyebrows. Some said she was of Cornish extraction. Others declared she came of Romany stock, that her grandmother had been a member of a gipsy tribe who had often spent summers on the moor. Whatever the truth was, she was different in several respects from other farmers' wives and had none of the easy manner and ready laughter of Jennifer's mother. Her daughters seemed half afraid of her and Jennifer had never heard either of them answer her back or refuse to do her bidding.

"You'll stay and have a bite of dinner with us?" she asked, handing Jennifer the glass of home-made wine.

"It's kind of you, but my father . . ."

"He'll not be home yet a while, I reckon. The mist's thick around Plymouth, so Harry Best told us when he dropped in a while back."

"Well, in that case, thank you. But can't I help?"

"You sit where you are and be comfortable. You don't want to spoil those nice soft hands."

To Jennifer's astonishment they ate dinner in the parlour instead of around the big kitchen table. Not in all the years she had been visiting Edgecombe Farm had she been entertained in this room, used only on special occasions such as weddings and funerals. As they filed in, she noticed that all of them, except Mrs Vicary, looked ill at ease and to her embarrassment, she found herself making polite conversation, just as she would have done at a luncheon party at Aunt Lucy's. Alice stared at her in amazement. Bertha began to giggle and was immediately shushed by her mother. Mr Vicary concentrated on his meal. In the hope of returning the situation to some kind of normality, Jennifer turned to Alan and discovered, to her further surprise, that he was regarding her with open admiration, listening to her aimless chatter as if she were uttering words of extreme wisdom. She wanted to cry out,

"For goodness' sake, let us stop all this nonsense! This is exactly what I have longed to escape from —the pretence, the stupid conventions, the empty talk."

Instead, it was her aunt's careful training which saved the situation. She found herself taking charge of the conversation, encouraging Mr Vicary to talk about farming, teasing Alice gently about admirers, praising Bertha's sampler on the wall above the side-board. But it was with a sense of relief that, soon after the meal was over and her offer to wash the dishes had been refused, Jennifer mounted her pony and started for home.

In the past, whenever she had been unhappy or disturbed, she would go to a special place which she had kept a secret, to sort out her feelings and thoughts. It was a little combe where a stream rippled quietly amongst green water-weed or fell in tiny waterfalls between ferny banks beneath a rowan tree. Grey wagtails flitted from rock to rock like graceful dancers and dragonflies hovered and darted over the water. There were many such places on the moor and she did not know what made this one so special. She had gone there often after the death of her mother, and on the day before she left for London. She had not thought the need would arise to go to the combe on her first day back but everything had turned out so differently from what she had expected. There had been the anticlimax and disappointment of her arrival when she had found her father was not there to welcome her. Then this morning she had been given the distressing news about the American who had rebuilt Heronslea and taken away some of the commoners' rights and part of Lidhead warren. Following which, Mollie had spoken those strange words which had sounded almost like a warning. She had tried to forget them, so certain had she been that nothing would have changed and that she could slip back into the old life without the slightest difficulty. But Mrs Vicary's attitude seemed to have borne out what Mollie had said, that she did not, in fact, belong tidily in one world as Mollie did, and Tom, and Ned Hext the wall-builder and Mollie's father, the warrener, and Aunt Lucy and her friends. But then, neither did Jennifer's father. And what about Alan? He had been born into the narrow world of the moorland farmer but he was ambitious and his schooling, when he had not only received an education but also mixed with boys from different backgrounds, had set him apart. But he had not been sent right away, to a totally different environment as she had been. What *had* London done for her, or *to* her?

Her thoughts confused, her joy at home-coming unexpectedly clouded, she decided to make a slight detour and spend a little while at her special place. It had never failed to bring comfort and peace of mind. She felt sure it would do so, now.

The combe lay on the other side of the turnpike road, in a cleft between two tors, about a mile and a half from her home. She turned the mare's head and rode into the valley of the Lid and crossed the river by the ford, then up the slope on the opposite side. Some mares with foals watched warily as she passed and sheep scattered on either side but the red Devon cattle, soon to be taken off the moor, went on placidly grazing. She saw one moorman looking over his stock and a few women and children picking whortleberries. But once on the crest of the hill she was alone with the larks, singing high overhead or flitting along in front of her. The sun shone from a blue sky from which all trace of mist had vanished. She breathed deeply of the heady moorland air, then let Bracken have her head. The gallop along the ridge was exhilarating and she began to feel calmer. Then, as she came out from behind an outcrop of rocks which had blocked her view, she pulled Bracken up so short that the mare was forced back on her haunches. For there, away to her right, was the new house of Heronslea.

It was like no other dwelling on the moor although she had seen houses—no, mansions, like it in London. It had the straight, elegant lines of Georgian architecture and was of such a gleaming whiteness that she knew now why Mollie had said it stood out for miles around. Work was still in progress at one end and even at this distance she could hear the sound of hammering. The rough ground to the left and on the hill above the house had been cleared and a number of men were working there, probably planting the trees Mollie had mentioned. The cleared ground seemed no more than the original holding of Heronslea, and that puzzled her for it did not seem to merit Mollie's outburst against the American.

Then she saw the wall. A typical Dartmoor wall, formed of granite boulders of every shape and size, it started from a point on the turnpike road, beside the little beech wood on the far side of Lidbridge, and ran in a straight line about half a mile to the east of the house, up over the slope of Hendown and disappeared over the horizon. In growing dismay, Jennifer looked westwards, and there was the other wall of the enclosure, beginning at the roadside just below her, crossing the marshy ground opposite and then, again following an inexorable line, climbing up towards Cock Tor. It dropped out of her line of vision on the far side of the tor but she saw that it continued to the high moor beyond. And just below the wall, *inside* the huge enclosure, was her special place.

"No!" she exclaimed aloud. "Oh, *no!*"

Dismay gave way to anger. She felt it boiling up inside her so that her cheeks grew hot and her fingers dug into her palms as she clenched her hands on the reins. Her secret refuge had been taken from her just as the commoners' rights had been wrested from them, by a foreigner, an American who had worked his cotton plantation with slave labour, and whom she had seen try to force a beautiful thor-

oughbred horse along a path it was too frightened
to take.

As she remembered that incident, in her mind
she echoed Mollie's words: "I wish it had thrown
him so heavily he'd broken his neck."

She turned Bracken's head and rode back the way
she had come, so that she would be out of sight of
that splendid mansion and the new walls which
spelled the end of freedom in this part of the moor.
But the anger remained, transmitting itself to her
mount so that the little mare, for the first time
played her up and baulked so sharply on the river
bank that Jennifer was all but thrown into the river.

She was still seething when she reached Lidden
Barton. At her summons, Zebedee came furtively,
glancing nervously towards the house.

"*Now* what are you frightened of?" she demanded, allowing her feelings to get the better of
her.

"The man," he mumbled.

"What man, for goodness' sake?"

He jerked his thumb over his shoulder. "The one
that be in there."

"My father?" She stared at him in astonishment.
"You can't be afraid of . . . But this means that
Papa is home?"

Without waiting for an answer, she tossed him
the reins. Then, clutching her skirt high to avoid
tripping in her haste, she ran across the yard and

into the house. The door of the study was ajar and she heard a movement inside.

"Papa!" she exclaimed. "Papa, I'm back! I'm home!" and went joyfully into the room.

Her father was not there. Instead, a stranger was standing beside the bookshelf. He was young, very tall, slimly built. His grey eyes were fringed with dark lashes, in contrast to the fairness of his hair. His handsome features were matched by the elegance of his clothes, for he wore a blue tail-coat and oatmeal-coloured trousers and his shirt had a frilled front. Used as Jennifer had become to the sombrely dressed men of Victorian London, his appearance was even more of a shock than Alan's had been. He seemed, in fact, to have stepped straight out of the world of dashing Regency bucks that she liked to read about. She felt a strange little shiver of excitement run up and down her spine and for a few moments it seemed as if she were mesmerized.

Then the young man spoke, in a slow drawling voice. "You are Miss Haslam?" he asked and sounded surprised. "Allow me to present myself. My name is Meares, Darrell Meares of Heronslea. Professor Haslam kindly suggested I might avail myself of his library."

For the first time she noticed the volume in his hand. It was one of her father's most precious books, a first edition, out of print.

"I don't believe you," she said. "No one, not even

my mother, has ever been allowed in Papa's study when he is not here."

"You are doubting my word?" he asked in haughty astonishment.

"Yes, I am. When I come upon a complete stranger, alone in my father's study, with one of my father's most valuable books in his hand . . ."

"Are you accusing me of stealing?" the young man demanded, flushing angrily.

"I think I would not be the first one to do that."

"How dare you!" He stepped forward threateningly. "How dare you speak to me in that way?"

For a moment she hesitated, then everything that had gone wrong that morning coalesced in anger against this man. Standing her ground, glaring up at him, she declared:

"I shall speak to you how I choose. You are not in Carolina now, and I am not one of your slaves to be treated . . ."

His voice was icy as he interrupted her. "I understood, Miss Haslam, that you had been sent to London to be turned into a lady. What a pity the plan did not succeed."

Placing the book carefully on the desk, he picked up his hat, and before Jennifer could recover from the shock of his words, had gone from the room.

She was so furious she had to grip the edge of the desk to stop her hands trembling. And she knew, although she thrust the thought away in a kind of panic, that part of her anger was due to the fact that in those few moments before the young man named himself, she had felt an extraordinary attraction towards him. It had been as startling as an electirc current, a reaction which no man, not even Alan, had ever aroused in her before.

~~~~~~~~~~~~~~~~~~~~~~~~~~~~~~~~~~~~~

Chapter Two

Professor Haslam was agitatedly polishing his spectacles as he looked up at Jennifer, standing beside his desk.

"Am I to understand that you actually accused Mr Meares of stealing?"

Her forefinger traced the tooling on his blotter and she thought inconsequentially, I am like Papa, I have to fiddle with something when I am worried. She was certainly worried now because her father's reaction was proving entirely different from what she had expected. She had left it until this morning to tell him about her encounter with the American, not wanting to spoil the happiness of their reunion on the previous evening.

"I thought I had every right to do so," she answered, seeking to justify her conduct in face of his seemingly condemnatory attitude. "I would ask you to realize, Papa, that I came upon a complete stranger here in your study where nobody—not even Mama when she was alive—has ever been allowed when you are not present and he had a book in his hand. This book," she added, thrusting it in front of her father's eyes. "You have often told me how precious it is."

"That is very true," he said, putting on his spectacles to peer at the spine.

"There you are, then," Jennifer declared triumphantly. "Wouldn't you expect me to have thought he was about to steal it, seeing that you would not lend such a book even to Mr Taverner, your closest friend? Besides, I already knew that Mr Meares was quite capable of theft, since he has stolen so much land."

Her father frowned. "Jennifer, my dear, I did hope that London might have cured you of exaggerating so freely. Mr Meares has not stolen any land. He has acquired it by lease from the Duchy, under the act of 1822."

"Papa, we all know what abuses that act led to. And Mr Taverner has given his opinion that the king had no right to pass such an act, and Mr Taverner is a parson and surely should know what he is talking about."

Sighing, her father laid his spectacles on the desk. She saw what she had first noticed last night, that he looked a good deal older than before she went away. He had lost weight and his grey hair was thin and wispy, and the veins on his hands were more prominent. She knelt beside him and took hold of his hand.

"Papa, pray let us not be at odds over this matter. Believe me, I acted in what I thought was in your interest."

"No, my dear." He was shaking his head and still looking disturbed. "I think that is not entirely the truth. I believe that you were already so incensed by what you heard about Mr Meares . . ."

"Not only by what I had heard. On my own account, I was angry because . . ." She caught herself up, for even were she to reveal the secret of her special place, she knew her father would not have understood. She said instead, "He told me you had given him the run of your library which I believed to be a downright lie."

"Those are strong words, Jennifer, but I must admit I had not expected him to take me quite so literally."

"You *have* offered to lend him books?"

"Yes, within limits. He appears to be genuinely interested in my subject. And what is more," he added, with satisfaction, "he has taken the greatest possible care not to damage any of the prehistoric remains which lie within his enclosures."

Jennifer rose to her feet. "That, naturally, would assure him of *your* favour."

"It certainly makes me more favourably disposed to him than I am to those farmers who have taken irreplaceable stones of great antiquity to be used as gate-posts or doorsteps."

"You would rather a man cared for sterile stones than for living people?" she demanded. Then, seeing her father's shocked expression, she said quickly, "I'm sorry, that was rude. But, Papa," she went on, striving to keep calm, "if you had only mentioned this Mr Meares in your letters . . ."

"Did I not do so?" he asked in surprise.

She shook her head. "You wrote of little else but your latest discoveries and theories."

"Then the remark you just made was justified." He sighed deeply, and began polishing his spectacles again. "I do bury myself in the past. I know that only too well, but on the whole I find the world of today beyond my comprehension. All this fuss and bad feeling over what amounts to no more than a few acres of rough ground . . ."

Jennifer was about to argue, then realized it would be useless. Her father was not rich but he never wanted for money. Nor had he ever had to wrest a living from a land in which nature often seemed bent on destroying every effort a man made to sustain himself and his family. It was from her mother that she had inherited her understanding of the moormen's difficulties, and later she had learned more about them from Alan and Mollie. On the other hand, her father's academic mind, preoccupied with the past, seemed incapable of even acknowledging that such problems existed.

"Let us forget about Mr Meares," she said, persuasively. "You have a great deal of work for me, Mrs Westcott said."

"Mrs Westcott? I thought she had gone away, because of somebody being ill."

"You are thinking of Ada, Papa. Her mother is ill. Mrs Westcott brought us in breakfast this morning."

"Did she?" He rubbed his chin. "So she did. I remember now, I congratulated her on getting my egg just right for once." He looked up at Jennifer with a rueful smile. "You can see I haven't changed, can't you?"

She kissed him affectionately. "Neither have I, despite Aunt Lucy's attempts to curb what she called my hot-headedness and self-will."

He patted her cheek. "I didn't want you changed, Jennifer. It just seemed to me that this London visit might be of benefit to you."

"I've no doubt it has been," she said gaily, "for it has shown me where I truly belong and that is here, on the moor. Now, where do you want me to start?"

He indicated a pile of papers which seemed in imminent danger of sliding off his desk. "If you would be kind enough to sort out all those notes and references and get them in order . . ."

She gathered up the papers, holding them firm with her chin. "I'd better take them into the parlour where there will be more space." At the door she turned to say in amusement, "How Aunt Lucy would disapprove if she knew we still call it the parlour. 'The withdrawing-room, my dear child, please,' " she corrected herself in a fair imitation of her aunt's voice. Then she saw that her father's head was bent over his desk and he was already immersed in a period when men lived in crude stone huts roofed with heather turves and there was no place at all where anyone could withdraw.

But as she was trying to close the door behind her with her foot, he looked up and said:

"Jennifer, I do think that Mr Meares should receive an apology. If you would just write . . ."

"You want *me* to apologize to *him*?" she asked. almost letting the pile of papers slip from her grasp.

"Do you not consider, if you are honest with yourself, that an apology is called for?"

The blood rushed into her cheeks, making them burn. "No, Papa, I do not. But if you order me to write to him, I will do so."

"I am not *ordering* you, child," her father said mildly, "and if it is so entirely against your inclination, then I will make it my duty to . . ."

"No, Papa, it is certainly not your duty. That I *do* know, even if I do not allow that it is mine, either. I will do as you wish and write to Mr Meares, explaining that there was a misunderstanding."

"Thank you, my dear. It will make matters easier when we meet. Just a short note will suffice and then Zebedee—I think that is the name of the poor half-witted boy I have lately noticed about the place —can take it."

"I do not think he will, Papa. He is too frightened of what he describes as a giant black man."

"That is merely Mr Meares' Negro butler. He is perfectly harmless."

"You mean that there really is a black man at Heronslea—a slave?"

"I should doubt that he is a slave," her father said, bending again to his work, "but in any case, Mr Meares' household arrangements are no concern of ours. My dear, I should be very grateful if you could deal with the notes on cromlechs and dolmens first. That is the material to be incorporated into my next chapter."

Jennifer crossed the hall to the parlour and dumped the papers into a chair. Then she found writing paper and pen and sat down to write the letter to Darrell Meares. Her first attempts ended up in the waste-paper basket and she was not completely satisfied with the final one. This did not surprise her, for nothing she wrote could express her true feelings. In what was supposed to be a note of apology, it would scarcely have been appropriate to describe the fury which still arose within her as she recalled the cutting words he had spoken to her before storming out of the house. Even now, although she still rankled at those words, was still angry with him on the commoners' account as well as her own, she could vividly remember the physical reaction he had roused in her, pleasurable and exciting. The memory troubled her, because her body had betrayed her into feeling attracted towards a man whose character appeared to be in direct contrast to the values she most admired and respected in the opposite sex.

Zebedee, as Jennifer had expected, was too terrified of the "black giant" to take her note to Heronslea, and she could not ask Mrs Westcott to do so. Apart from the fact that, with Ada away, the housekeeper was fully occupied, it was a mile to the entrance gates and another mile up the drive to the house. In the event, Jennifer had no option but to deliver the note herself. Reluctantly, that afternoon, she set out on Bracken.

When she reached the bridge, she found Ned Hext there, leaning on the parapet, and reined in to greet him. Ned, almost seventy now, was the finest builder of stone walls in this part of the moor. In her childhood Jennifer had spent many happy hours watching him at work and listening to his stories. Sometimes he would recite poetry to her, simple lines of his own creating, full of the grandeur and mystery of the moor which he loved.

"Why, if 'tisn't Miss Jenny!" he exclaimed delightedly, clasping the hand she held out to him. " 'Tis wunnerful good to see 'ee again. So they couldn't keep 'ee in London, then?"

"No, indeed. I longed to be back. But I didn't expect to see such a change. All this . . ." She gestured towards the big white house and the new walls. "Did you help to build the enclosure?"

"I did not." His tone of voice matched his grim expression. "Leastways, not after the first day. The 'foreigner' brought in a gang of Irishmen who'd no notion of how to build a wall properly. 'Twill not last above twenty years, I don't reckon, and there are some places where 'twould only take a pony leaning 'pon it to push un over."

His speech became broader as he grew more indignant. Jennifer, although sympathizing with his contempt for poor workmanship, was amused at his use of the term "Irishmen". There *had* been Irishmen at one time on the moor, astonishing the moormen by wearing no shoes or socks, but now the word could apply equally to Cornishmen or any other labourers who came from "outalong".

"Speaking of ponies," Ned went on, "that be a nice little mare you'm riding."

"Yes, isn't she? Alan Vicary gave her to me."

"Did he, now? Nan Webber'll not be pleased about that, I reckon."

"Why not?"

"Telling everyone that Alan's her sweetheart, she is."

"But she's . . ." Jennifer was about to remark that Nan was only a giggly girl with scarcely a sensible thought in her head. Then she realized that Nan must be eighteen now, and two years might have made a great deal of difference. But Alan's sweetheart? Surely not, considering the way he had behaved since her return, the hints that he regarded her, Jennifer, as part of his future? She put the thought firmly aside and said:

"I must be on my way, Ned. I'll be seeing you around, I expect."

She was about to move off when he put a restraining hand on the rein. "I'd like to give 'ee a word of warning, Miss Jenny. I've tried with your father but he don't really listen half the time, unless 'tis talk about those old stones he's so determined I shan't use in my walls. 'Tis concerning that lad that's been taken on at your place."

"Zebedee? Why should you want to warn me against him?"

"Not *against* him. 'Tis on his own account I'd advise you to keep an eye on him. 'Tis this way. You know how folks have their own favourite place for picking 'hurts' when they'm in season."

"Whortleberries? Yes, I do know that."

"Zebedee's family has always favoured a little combe upalong," Ned pointed towards the hill to the east of Heronslea. "He've been going there with his mother and sisters since he were a toddler, and you do know, Miss Jenny, how the villagers will come from miles away for the picking, making a real treat of it besides the bit of extra money they do collect by selling the surplus above their own needs. This year, a few weeks back, 'twas, Zebedee's family came as usual—as merry as a flock of finches —and what did they find but the new wall blocking their way and notices to keep out, writ bold and clear?"

"You mean their favourite place is on Mr Meares' property?"

"That's right. Well, the women were disappointed of course but they moved on and filled their cans and baskets elsewhere. But Zebedee—he'm a bit mizzy-maazy as I dare say you've seen already, and he don't understand about leases and property rights and sich like . . ."

"No more do I," said Jennifer fiercely. "Not when it comes to overriding commoners' rights and acquiring land which has been rented by the same family for generations."

Ned regarded her admiringly. "My, but London's not damped your spirit! Course, there be many of us do feel that way, too, and some as are prepared to take matters into their own hands, but that lad— well, he's likely to get hurt."

"In what way?"

"If he do go trepassing—for whatever folks like us think, that's how the American would regard it —and get caught, I reckon he'd get a beating, if not worse."

"From Mr Meares?"

"Him or one of his men. He've a whole gang of tin miners working for him, them as was thrown out of work a while back, and I don't need to tell you they'm a purty rough lot."

She said, frowning, "I'll certainly warn Zebedee and try to make him understand. I know," she added with sudden inspiration, "I'll tell him he's likely to run into the black man anywhere inside the enclosures. That will frighten him away. Thank you for telling me, Ned. By the way, what did you mean when you said that there are some people prepared to take matters into their own hands—regarding the enclosures, I mean?"

He averted his eyes and let go of the rein. "You —you must have misheard me, Miss Jenny," he said evasively. "After all, there be nothing moor folk can do, be there?"

She was sure she had not misheard him but she knew it was no good pursuing the subject. If the moormen had some plan for opposing Darrell Meares, they would keep it secret. In the past, Ned, with some coaxing, might have told her. Now, she doubted if he would and it was perhaps better that he should not do so. She had been nearly two years in London, which to the moormen was "foreign parts", and living a life which they might think set her apart from them for it was the kind of life which in their eyes must seem much more akin to that of the rich American.

She could feel Ned watching her as she rode away and suddenly she realized that once she was clear of the clump of beeches, he would have an uninterrupted view of her riding up the drive to Heronslea.

"Into the camp of the enemy," she said aloud, dramatically.

She hesitated, only too eager to find some excuse for not delivering the note after all. But there was her father to consider.

A little ahead of her one of the village boys was scuffing his way along the highway. Despite the fact that he seemed to have doubled his height, she recognized him as the midwife's son. Here, surely, was her solution.

She called to the boy and a few minutes later, hidden by the beech trees, handed him her note to Darrell Meares, and a shilling piece, and sent him on his way to Heronslea. Then she turned off the road and, making sure she was visible to Ned Hext, rode leisurely up a track in the opposite direction.

Alan leaned on the gate of his father's top field, reflectively chewing a blade of grass. Beside him sat his collie bitch, tongue lolling, eyes fixed unwaveringly on her master's face. The sun was setting behind them like a huge orange plate balanced on the rim of the hill. Across the valley the moor was illumined by its rays, the dark firs of a plantation a sharp contrast to the yellow and tawny hues of grass and bracken. The starkness of the granite tors was muted into soft shades of grey and lilac. At the foot of the hill the river had a golden glint.

Alan's mind was not on the view or the beauty of this perfect evening. His absorption was with a piece of land in the valley directly below him, a holding which must surely come vacant before long. It was good land, for the most part in small rectangular fields enclosed by stone walls, and sheltered by the encircling hills and a windbreak of trees. By careful treatment with lime and sea-sand it should yield satisfactory crops of corn and wheat, turnips and potatoes. There was easy access to water and the cornmill was nearby. At present the fields supported only a few South Devon cattle and the surrounding ground was grazed by ponies left to breed indiscriminately, without any thought being given to selection and improvement. Ben Cobbledick who farmed the land was almost ninety, a childless widower who had held on to his home tenaciously, declaring that when the time came he would die in the bed in which he had been born. He had even threatened to turn his gun on anyone who tried to carry him off to some charitable institution which would mean the end of independence.

The cottage which went with the land was built of moorstone like every other dwelling in the neighbourhood. It was small but there was no reason why it could not be enlarged. There was a good spring which never dried up, space for more outbuildings, and a bit of ground, now choked with nettles, which would make a fair-sized vegetable garden. Besides which, for an incoming tenant, there would be the extra acres of the newtake. In Alan's opinion the place ideally fitted the requirements of an ambitious young farmer starting up on his own. He could manage the rent unless the Duchy increased it exorbitantly. His father would let him have a couple of mares served by his best stallion. His mother would provide some laying pullets and a cockerel and some odds and ends of furniture. That was all they could do for him, they had said, having the two girls to provide for. If things worked out as he planned, he would need no more help from them than that.

There had been two choices open to him and he had weighed one against the other during the past year. Nan Webber, youngest daughter of a farmer over beyond Dartmeet, fair, plump, with bold blue eyes, would marry him tomorrow if he asked her. Once or twice he had considered the idea, egged on by his mother, but always his thoughts had returned to Jennifer Haslam. Now she was home again, prettier than ever, very smart in her fine clothes, yet acting as if she had been away for no more than a month instead of this long time. He had known, within five minutes of meeting her at the inn at Moretonhampstead, that there were no longer two choices. He wanted Jenny for his wife, and no other. He supposed that deep down he had known it must be so, for he had loved her for as long as he could remember. Before she went to London it had been the love of a boy for the girl he had known since childhood. Now, seeing her again, her figure no longer that of a girl, her voice and manner showing the poise she had acquired in London, he had known desire so strong it had kept him wakeful most of the night, for there had been anxiety too. His fear was that she would set her sights much higher now than she had done two years ago. There was, for instance, the American over at Heronslea. A rich young bachelor who had built himself a fine house like that must surely be in search of a wife, and who more suitable than Jenny, born on the moor yet belonging to the gentry on her father's side, young and pretty and vivacious, with almost two years' tuition by her aunt in London in the ways which would fit her for being mistress of Heronslea?

The collie turned her head, then pressed herself close to her master as Mrs Vicary joined them. She had never actually ill-treated the bitch but her attitude to animals was entirely practical. She never fondled or petted them, but neither had she made any fuss of her two daughters, even when they were babies, having little time for her own sex. The fact that she set Alan's interests before theirs, even before her husband's, had long been accepted by every member of the family.

She said, "You got your eye on Ben's property?"

Alan nodded without speaking. He was not anxious to bring his thoughts out into the open.

" 'Twould suit you and Nan Webber a fair treat.

She'd get that cottage into shape in no time. A good worker is Nan, strong, too, and built for easy childbearing."

"I'm not thinking of choosing a wife as I would a beast," he said.

She looked at him, eyes narrowed. "You'm not thinking in other directions, I hope?"

He tried to stave her off. "I don't know what you mean."

"Oh yes, you do. Jenny Haslam is what I do mean."

He shrugged. "What if I am?"

She put a hand on his arm. " 'Twill do you no good, Alan. She's not cut out for a farmer's wife."

"Her mother came from farming stock. Jenny's knowledgeable about animals and she's not afraid of work."

His mother's tone was scornful. "Didn't you notice her hands? She's not done a day's work this last two years, I'll be bound."

"You can't blame her for that," he retorted hotly. "It wasn't Jenny's wish to go to London and lead an idle life. Now she's back again . . ."

"She'll keep on that housekeeper, and Ada—*and* they've a boy to do the outside work."

"Jenny keeps busy in other ways. She does a lot of work for her father."

"Huh! Scratching away with a pen isn't going to get babies fed and floors scrubbed."

"Oh, give over, mother!" he exclaimed impatiently, then turned to face her. "I suppose this is the reason you acted so strangely, setting dinner in the parlour."

"She'd not have expected to eat in the kitchen, not after . . ."

"Of course she would! Anybody could see she was put out about it, made to feel like a stranger instead . . ."

"She is a stranger, Alan, to our ways. She'm a cut above us, and well you do know it even if you won't admit it. A man who sets his sights too high can do himself a power of harm. I'd not want to see you hurt."

Alan thrust up his chin. "Mother, I'm not a child. I don't need protecting. In any case, I'm more concerned that I might not be able to make Jenny happy than any hurt she could do to me. I love her. I reckon I always have done and always will. Whether she'll take me or not, I don't know, but whatever the odds, I mean to try."

His mother's eyes searched his face and he saw her expression change from disapproval to a kind of unwilling admiration. After a few moments she shrugged and turned away.

"Reckon I'd best accept it, then, and do what I can to help you."

"I don't *want* help, Mother, except for you to treat Jenny no different from what you did before she went away. In any case," he added, smiling to soften the words, "there's nothing you *could* do, is there?"

She was staring down into the valley, her gaze fixed thoughtfully on Ben Cobbledick's property.

"There *are* ways," she said, almost to herself. Her face had the dark, closed look which made him wonder if the rumour that she had gipsy blood in her veins was true.

"Mother?" he said, suddenly made anxious.

She turned back to him, smiling. " 'Tis time we went in. The girls will have got supper ready by now."

He questioned her as they walked towards the house but she would give no hint of what she had meant. The next morning, as he was turning the cows out after milking, he saw her in the distance, making her way along a twisting sheep track towards Gibbet Tor. On the far side of the tor, he remembered, in a tumbledown hovel beside a thicket of stunted oaks, lived old Hannah Sculpher. And she, it was reputed, was a notable black witch.

The morning was dull and cold, with a sharp breeze blowing off the high moor. Darrell shivered as he rode out to inspect the work being done on his enclosures. In such weather as this, when the landscape appeared bleak and drab, the bracken soggy with rain and the tors dark and hostile, he wished he was back in South Carolina, about to ride through the green acres of the plantation where

Negro women would be working with brightly
coloured kerchiefs around their heads, chattering
to each other as they moved along the rows of
cotton bushes, filling the baskets on their backs. Instead, he would be greeted by the sullen faces of
the tin miners he had engaged to plant the thousands of young trees, both conifers and soft-woods,
on the dark peaty soil that had been cleared above
and on the western side of the house. They were
unskilled in work on the land and their efforts were
clumsy and unsatisfactory. Either they put the sap-
lings in too deep or he would find them almost on
the surface, their roots exposed to sun and wind.
Instead of appearing to be so discontented, he considered these labourers should have been grateful
to him for finding them employment after the
closure of Wheal Becka. They and their families
could have come near to starvation but for him.

And *that* was something those who criticised him
for being a slave-owner might remember. On his
father's plantation, as on many others, the Negroes
had been housed, fed, given medical treatment
when necessary and pensioned off when they became too old to work. Could that be said of the
workers in any of the industrial towns he had seen
on his travels through England? And was the life
of a savage in the African jungle so idyllic that to
have it exchanged for work in a climate which
suited him, so dreadful?

Of course there were abuses, of course there

were cruel masters and harsh overseers, and the conditions in which the slaves were shipped across the ocean left much to be desired. But so did conditions in English mills and mines, with their scandalous employment of child labour. They were hypocrites, the English, he considered, with their outward show of piety, and they had no right to condemn a system about which they knew so little, unless they first put their own house in order. Even those ladies who held meetings and asked for subscriptions to help the abolitionists in the northern states of America doubtless continued to wear cotton garments without a second thought. Did they ever stop to consider that cotton could not be produced on any considerable scale without the labour of countless workers imported from Africa? In the past there had been a movement towards the gradual emancipation of the slaves but then had come the invention of the cotton gin which had so speeded up the process of removing the seed from the cotton and opened up opportunities for immense profits in the Southern states. That had meant an increase in the slave trade. But now the Northern states were becoming vociferous in the cause of abolition, although from what Darrell could gather, from correspondents who wrote him from America, there were political as well as humanitarian motives behind these outbursts.

Such problems, however, were no longer his affair. He had enough of his own here on Dartmoor where, on an impulse he was already regretting, he had thought to tame a wilderness just as his forefathers had done in Carolina. And he could do it, he felt sure, if only he were left alone to carry out his plans. Instead, he had difficulties to contend with quite apart from those of climate and terrain which he had taken into account. There was the opposition of the moormen who ranted on about their trivial rights over a few acres of rough grazing, and of the warrener who stood to lose a few dozen rabbits. If such things made so great a difference to their lives, they had only themselves to blame, for having so little initiative and ambition. Such men deserved to go to the wall and make room for those who were prepared to use the land to its best advantage. And were not trees badly needed after the depletion of the timber stock during the Napoleonic wars? He was providing employment, not reducing it, and that was exactly what he intended to tell that impudent young daughter of Professor Haslam when next they met.

He had not been deceived by the note which had been delivered to him on the previous day. It was in no way an apology for her angry outburst and the accusation that she had caught him in the act of stealing one of her father's books. Reading between the lines, he had guessed that the letter had been written under duress from her father when he heard about the incident. If she *had* apologized, he would have done the same, for admittedly he had gone beyond the bounds of politeness in his final remark. As it was, he considered, as he had done at the time, that it was no more than she deserved.

He had rarely been more astonished than by his meeting with Jennifer Haslam. From the way her father had spoken of her, telling him how unusually intelligent she was and what a help she had been in his work, he had built up a picture of a quiet, rather grave-mannered girl who found London not to her liking because it was too raffish. Instead, he had been confronted by a black-haired little spitfire, clutching her muddied skirt so high that he had caught sight of her white stockings above her riding boots. If she had been one of his own sisters he would have given her a good spanking, just as he had done when Lucilla had . . .

"Stop that!" he told himself, angrily slapping his whip against his boot. "Stop harking back to the past, to Carolina, to home. You've chosen this new life and you've got to make a success of it. You needed something to occupy your mind and tire your body so that you could sleep at night. Now you've found it. What more do you want?"

A great deal more, came his unwilling answer. A very great deal more.

He had been riding with his head down, deep in thought. Now he raised it as he heard shouting, then the thud of hooves from further up the hill. Half a dozen wild ponies were careering around amongst his newly planted trees. The miners were downing tools and running towards the ponies, only too ready to take advantage of the diversion.

"Stay where you are, damn you!" Darrell shouted. "You'll only make things worse."

He galloped up the hill towards two men who were yelling wildly and throwing their arms about in a fruitless attempt to drive the ponies back through a gap in the wall.

"Stand still, you fools!" he ordered. "Those animals will be completely unmanageable if you get them in a panic. One of you, stand beside that boulder, and the other, get nearer the wall and don't close in until I say so."

The chestnut played him up, cavorting like a dancer, fighting for its head, and not for the first time he wished he had made a different choice of mount. This highly bred creature with its slender legs and nervous disposition, he was discovering, was not suited to the requirements of rough moorland riding. When the wild ponies had settled to grazing again in a tight little group, he edged forward, gesturing to the men to do the same. Controlling his own impatience as well as that of his mount, he drove the intruders quietly towards the gap. He had them within a few yards, going willingly now that they had seen their way of escape, when a boy appeared in the gap. Startled, the ponies turned back on themselves and scattered wildly, trampling more young trees.

Darrell swore furiously and spurred forward, his

whip raised. The boy fled, keeping close to the wall, with Darrell after him. Just as Darrell was within reach and was leaning down to grab a shoulder, the lad scrambled over the wall and dropped lightly into the enclosure. The two workmen, at Darrell's command, went after him. The boy turned for a moment, revealing a moon-like face, then set off again, turning and twisting like a hare. Darrell could hear his cackling, foolish laughter.

There was a man replacing stones which had fallen from the wall further up the hill. If he kept out of sight, there might still be a chance to catch the boy and teach him a lesson he would not forget in a hurry. Darrell rode back down the hill and into the enclosure and then up again. The boy, seeing him, scrambled up and over the wall.

"Catch him!" Darrell shouted. "You there, by the wall, catch that boy!"

The man moved swiftly and the lad, taken by surprise, hesitated, then started downhill. He was tiring now, and careless of direction. Then, abruptly, he stopped and looked up towards the ridge of the hill. Above the clamour and shouting men and thudding hooves came a girl's voice, and down the hill at full stretch on a sure-footed moorland pony came Jennifer Haslam. The workman threw himself on the boy and pinned him to the ground. The next moment the girl had reined in beside them and was setting about the man with her whip.

Anger made Darrell reckless. He put his horse at

the wall. For one breathtaking moment he thought the chestnut would not clear it. Then they were over. Snatching the whip from the girl's hand, he allowed his fury to explode into words, while the boy squirmed in the workman's grip and made strange little whimpering sounds more like those of a frightened animal than a human being.

When Darrell paused for breath the girl asked icily, "Have you quite finished?"

Tight-lipped, he made no answer. She said, "Perhaps, if you could control yourself, Mr Meares, I should understand why you are ill-treating this boy."

"It is no affair of yours," he retorted.

"Indeed it is. Zebedee is employed by my father."

Looking more closely at the lad, Darrell saw that he was in fact the half-witted youth who always slipped out of sight whenever he himself appeared at Lidden Barton.

"Very well, then," he said reluctantly. "I will enlighten you. He drove some ponies on to my land. They have damaged the trees I have planted. No doubt *that* was his intention."

"Is that true, Zebedee?" the girl asked. "Did you . . . ?"

"Are you questioning my word, Miss Haslam?" Darrell broke in.

"I am questioning Zebedee, or at least trying to do so. As I understand the law, anyone accused of a crime—if indeed this could be described as a crime—is given the chance to answer for himself. Did you drive those ponies on to Mr Meares' land, or what he believes is his land, Zebedee?"

The boy shook his head, his eyes wild with terror.

"You see?" Jennifer said triumphantly.

Darrell's voice was tight with anger. "You believe *his* word, against mine?"

"Did you actually see him *driving* the ponies?"

Taken aback, Darrell hesitated, then said quickly, "What I did see, and my men also, was this boy appearing in a gap in the wall which was obviously the way the ponies gained access."

"Appearing suddenly in a gap in the wall," Jennifer repeated scornfully. "Is that a crime to be punished by being hounded like a hare?"

"He meant to . . ."

"How do you know what he intended? I doubt if *he* does, half the time. You can surely see that poor Zebedee is . . ."

"Poor Zebedee!" he exclaimed wrathfully. "So I am to pity him and make allowances . . ."

"Certainly. You took away his whortleberries."

He stared at her in blank astonishment. "I— *what*?"

"Those," she said, pointing to some low bushes, "are whortleberries. Every summer people come from miles around to pick them and each family has its favourite place. To be honest, I don't suppose the fruit is really all that better in one spot than another but the villagers regard the picking as

the chance of a day out and so they have their pref-
erences. And Zebedee . . . But what's the use of my
trying to explain if you won't even listen?"

He had turned abruptly away, to hide the sudden
hurt her words had dealt him. Instead of this bleak
stretch of moorland, he was seeing the rioting colours of Carolina. He was seeing his young sisters,
reaching for the clusters of wild grapes, Lucilla begging their negress nurse to lift her higher, higher,
because there was one special branch which, she
was sure, would prove more luscious than the rest.

As always, he pushed memory from his mind and
said coldly, "Perhaps you will recollect, Miss Haslam, that is exactly what I said to you, when you
accused me of stealing one of your father's books."

"Oh, surely that is over and done with," she continued. "I did write you . . ."

"A very stilted note, which was in no way an
apology."

"Did you expect me to apologize after what you
said to me?"

He saw that the man still holding the boy was
listening with great interest to the conversation.
"Oh, let him go!" he ordered irritably, "and get back
to your work. *And* take that grin off your face or it
will be the worse for you."

Reluctantly, the man released Zebedee who
raced off down the hill.

The girl said, "I would be obliged if you would
give me back my whip. Not that I need it for my

mare but it might prove useful as protection against the ruffians you have brought amongst us—even against you, for that matter," she added, pointedly rubbing her wrist.

"You know perfectly well I would not do you any harm." He handed her back the ivory-handled whip and said stiffly, "I am sorry if I handled you roughly but you made me lose my temper."

"You had lost it before I came on the scene. I was on the far side of the ridge when I heard you shouting." She glanced towards the wall. The ponies had left the enclosure and were quietly grazing further away. "If you had to be so cross it should have been with your own men for such poor workmanship. *I* could build a better wall than that. Why, Ned Hext was saying only yesterday . . ."

"Who, pray, is Ned Hext?"

"The best builder of newtake walls in this quarter of the moor. And he writes poetry. But he'd not build walls for you whatever you offered him."

"And why is that?" he asked as she started to move off.

"Because he's a moorman and he'd not help you against his own kind. You know, you should not let that thoroughbred stand about in this cold wind when he's sweating."

He had been about to follow her, in order to try to teach her some sense and some manners. But after this latest effrontery to his pride he changed his mind. He wheeled the chestnut and rode back to the enclosure, his temper not improved by seeing that every man in the plantation of trees had stopped work to enjoy this unexpected entertainment. He rode among them, shouting and cursing and raising his whip threateningly, just as if he were one of the worst type of overseer on the cotton fields. But it was not against the ex-miners that his wrath was truly directed. It was against that damned slip of a girl who had the nerve to think she knew better than he did, about walls and horses and—just about everything it seemed.

Chapter Three

Alan, cutting peat on his father's "tie", became aware of the distressed lowing of cattle in the valley below. He straightened up and listened intently, a hand cupping his ear, for there was a stiff breeze blowing across the moor, rustling the heather stalks. Then he walked along the ridge until he could look down into the valley. Ben Cobbledick's cows were gathered by the gate leading to the shippon where they were milked. And it was long past milking time.

His first thought was for the beasts in trouble as he started down the hill. Ten minutes later he had opened the gate, let the cows into the yard and was calling for Ben. There was no response, only the noisy lowing of the cows and the barking of Ben's dog, tied up by its makeshift kennel. Seeing the back door open, Alan went into the cottage and called again. Still getting no reply, he glanced into each of the small rooms and found them empty.

He went back into the yard, decided Ben must have been delayed on some errand, and that the best thing he could do was to get on with the milking.

The cows had filed into the shippon, each making for its own stall post. Alan tethered the first one, then looked round for a pail. And then he saw Ben.

The old man was lying on the floor in an unnatural position, beside him a heap of scattered brushwood and broken hedge poles. A glance upwards told Alan what had happened. The old-fashioned "braith" floor of the loft had given way and Ben had fallen through the hole. Alan dropped to his knees, beside Ben, loosening his collar, feeling for a heart-beat. But even in the half-light of the shippon, one look at the old man's face was enough to tell him all he needed to know.

He was still kneeling there, shocked into immobility, when he heard Jennifer's voice.

"Alan? Alan, what's happened? I heard Ben's cows, then saw you running down the hill. I . . . Oh!"

Alan stood up slowly, hands hanging at his sides. "He's—he's dead. He fell from the tallet, you can see where the floor gave way. I—I think his neck is broken which means he . . . it must have been immediate, I mean, he didn't lie here—waiting for help, and no one coming."

Jennifer asked in a whisper, "What ought we to do? He should be moved, shouldn't he, and someone told . . . ?"

"Who is there to tell? He had no one, never wanted anyone after his wife died all those years ago."

"The doctor, then? I'll ride and fetch him, *and* Mr Taverner. There'll need to be a parson, to see to . . . Oh, Alan, how dreadful!"

When she began to cry he went to her and put his arms about her. "It's how he'd have wanted to go, Jenny, quickly, and on his own place. He was always so afeared of being taken away if he became too old and frail to manage."

"Yes, you're right. It's just that . . ." She gulped back her tears and tried to smile. "I've not been home more than a few days but the things that have happened . . ." The mournful lowing of the cows drowned her next words.

"I'd best get on and milk them," Alan said, "seeing there's nothing I can do for Ben. If you're sure you don't mind riding to . . ."

"I'll go at once. I think I know where to find Dr Harris. I passed him on my way over, making towards Laughter Hole. Mrs Westcott told me young Sam Brimacombe has bronchitis, I expect that's where he's gone."

"Good girl," he said approvingly. "How wrong my mother is when she says . . ." He stopped short, appalled by the thought which had come to him as he recalled the conversation with his mother. She had said she would do what she could to help him and when questioned had answered cryptically,

"There *are* ways." Next morning he had seen her taking a path in the direction of Hannah Sculpher's hovel. And old Hannah was supposed to be a black witch with the power of "over-looking" beasts so that they sickened and died, and who, it was said, stuck pins into effigies of humans on whom she wished ill.

"*No,*" he said aloud, "no, it can't be that!" and saw Jennifer's startled face as she turned back on her way to the yard.

"What is it?" she called. "You sounded— frightened, almost."

"It's all right," he answered quickly. "Just— something I thought of. It's not important."

Reassured, she mounted Bracken and rode off. Alan took off his coat and covered Ben's body. Then he set about milking. The feel of the cow's warm flank against his cheek, the steady swish of the milk spurting into the pail, calmed him, but the terrible suspicion still lurked at the back of his mind. Whether it would be better to question his mother or leave well alone, was a decision he shrank from making.

Mollie looked at her friend in open admiration when Jennifer recounted how she had gone to Zebedee's rescue. "Weren't you frightened, Jenny?"

"Yes, a little. After all, I was alone on the moor and Mr Meares' horse could outdistance Bracken easily unless I'd gone up amongst the clitter below

Cock Tor. Also, he had several men within call, apart from the one who had grabbed Zebedee. But I was angry, you see. Of course, he was angry, too, and he wrenched the whip from my hand in a very rough way but all the same . . . I didn't believe he would really do me any harm and once I realised that I felt I had a—a kind of power over him. I've never felt quite like that before. It was almost— exciting."

"*Exciting?* I don't know how you can say that. I should have been terrified. But then, I could not have brought myself to confront him in the first place."

"It *is* different for you, isn't it? I mean, you're involved, because of your father. If *you* annoyed him and he chose to be vindictive, he could probably get a lease on even more of the warren. I had nothing to lose."

"What about *your* father, though? Your house is Duchy property, don't forget."

Jennifer stared at her in astonishment. "You can't really imagine that the American would go that far? For one thing, he and Papa are friends, although, of course, Mr Meares has only to do some damage to that kistvaen up near Hen Tor and Papa would take a very different attitude." She broke off, deep in thought.

Mollie asked, "Now what are you thinking up? Jenny, you wouldn't deliberately damage . . . ?"

"No," she replied firmly. "I'm quite as anxious as

Papa is to preserve prehistoric remains—only I don't happen, like he does, to put them before human beings."

"So what can you do, if anything?"

"I've been thinking about that. I shall go and see Mr Ashworthy."

"The Forest reeve?" Mollie's voice held awe. "But, Jenny, it has to be something very important before you can put a case before him."

"*Isn't* this important? It certainly is to your father, and to the commoners with grazing rights on that land, even to poor Zebedee who wanted to pick whortleberries there." She laughed suddenly. "I do wish you could have seen the American's face when I spoke about that. I don't think he had the least idea what I was talking about."

Mollie said seriously, "Are you sure you're wise? The Duchy has granted Mr Meares a lease on this land. They're not likely to take it away from him now he's done so much clearance and his house is almost finished. And I doubt if the Forest reeve would have much say in a matter where such a big acreage, and therefore a substantial rent, is involved. In any case, isn't it possible that it could make Mr Meares so angry that he *would* be vindictive? Your father's lease does have to be renewed before long. You told me it was one of the things you had to remind him about."

For a moment Jennifer's resolve weakened. Then she said, "I'd have an answer ready if he tried that.

When I was in London I met a young man who—who admired me very much. In fact, I think he would have made an offer of marriage if I had given him the least encouragement. He worked on a big newspaper and I am sure that he would be delighted to receive a story about a scandal on Dartmoor. Can't you imagine the headlines? *Internationally famed archaeologist turned out of his home because of his daughter's fight on behalf of the commoners against a wealthy and ruthless American.*"

"Jenny, you can't be serious!" Mollie looked alarmed. "This is a matter involving the Duchy of Cornwall and Crown property. Surely you can't have forgotten that?"

"Yes, I had for the moment," Jennifer admitted. "I suppose I'm exaggerating as usual. But I do mean to oppose Mr Meares by some means or other, although . . ." She hesitated, then went on quickly, not looking at her friend, "although I do find him rather—attractive. If it weren't for this enclosure affair, I could . . ." She rose, twitching at her skirt. "Isn't it tiresome? Aunt Lucy was continually introducing me to eligible and what she considered highly suitable young men and I couldn't arouse any real interest in any of them. Yet now, a man whose character seems to be the exact opposite of everything I admire . . ."

"You mean you're falling in love with him?" asked Mollie incredulously as Jennifer broke off.

Jennifer stared down at the floor. "No. No, it

can't be that. It's just that—I don't really know how to describe it but each time we've met, despite our both being angry, I . . . Perhaps it was *because* we were angry," she went on with a shaky laugh. "Perhaps that created some sort of electric current between us. All I know is that I felt something I've never experienced before. Mollie, you're married. Is that what it feels like, when you and Tom . . . ?"

"Good gracious, no!" declared her friend in a shocked voice. "And I'd rather not talk about it. After all, it should be private, shouldn't it, between husband and wife?"

"Yes, I suppose so. I'm sorry, I shouldn't have asked. Only, I'm . . . Oh, well, it doesn't matter. I expect the next time I meet Mr Meares I shall decide I hate the very air he breathes and no two ways about it."

As Jennifer was about to leave, Mollie asked, "What about Alan?"

"I was thinking that if you have this feeling about the American . . . You told me you believed you could take up with Alan where you left off before you went to London. I hope you're not thinking of telling *him* that you find the American attractive."

"Of course not, silly. Anyway, Alan isn't interested in Mr Meares, his family not being involved in the controversy."

"Which is just as well. Alan has enough to worry him already."

"In what way?"

"Surely you've heard what's being said, about Ben Cobbledick's death?"

"I've heard nothing. *What* is being said?"

"That . . . Well, everyone knew that Alan had his eye on old Ben's farm, and you know there are always some people who like to be malicious and spread a rumour . . ."

"Mollie, what *are* you talking about?"

"There's talk going round that old Ben's death might not have been an accident."

"Of course it was an accident. I saw for myself . . ."

"What exactly did you see, Jenny?"

"Alan kneeling over Ben's body, trying to . . . Mollie, you surely can't mean . . . ? Nobody could believe that Alan, of all people . . . He's the kindest, most thoughtful person and . . . Oh, this is downright wicked!"

"Then you'd better go and tell Alan so," Mollie suggested. "If he thinks you've heard this rumour and have kept away . . ."

Jennifer stared at her friend, finding it difficult to take in what Mollie was implying. Then she went swiftly from the cottage, mounted Bracken and set off headlong for Edgecombe Farm.

Mrs Vicary was coming out of the hen house carrying a pail of eggs.

"Alan's upalong," she told Jennifer, "looking over the sheep. Would you like to come inside and wait for him?"

Jennifer hesitated, then said. "I think I'll ride up and meet him."

"Just as you like. You'll come in for a cup of tea afterwards? I won't put you in the parlour this time."

Jennifer smiled at her. "I'm glad. I'm sure you meant it kindly, Mrs Vicary, but I did feel rather embarrassed, being treated like a special visitor instead of one of the family."

Alan's mother gave Jennifer a thoughtful look. "Is that how you do feel—one of the family?"

"You've always made me so welcome." Disturbed by the way the older woman was regarding her, she added uncertainly, "It's—it's just a figure of speech anyway, isn't it?"

"I reckon Alan'd hope it meant something more."

"Well, yes, perhaps . . . I'll go and find him, anyway."

He was on a ridge above one of the deep combes, whistling directions to his collie bitch. Jennifer hung back, waiting until the sheep were under control, then she joined him.

"I've just come from Mollie's," she said at once. "She told me of this absurd rumour that's been put about. Who could have started anything so wicked?"

His face took on an unfamiliar closed look as he said, "I've my own idea about that."

"And you're not prepared to tell me?"

He hesitated, then said hesitantly, " 'Tis a bit

awkward, Jenny. You see . . . well, maybe you've heard another rumour, too, about me and . . ."

"Nan Webber," she broke in, with sudden inspiration. "Ned Hext told me Nan had been putting it about that she was your sweetheart. Is she, Alan?"

"You know very well that she isn't. I admit I've walked her out a time or two while you've been away but you'd not have expected me to live like a hermit, would you? From what you wrote, there was no lack of young gentlemen who . . ."

"You don't have to explain, Alan. You had every right to meet Nan or anyone else. I had no claim on you any more than you did on me. We just agreed, didn't we, that when I came back, if we felt—well, the same as before I went away . . ."

As her voice trailed away, he said, "That's just it. I'm not sure how you do feel. Anyway, there's no point in speaking of that at present. I'd been making such plans but now . . ."

"Plans for taking over Ben Cobbledick's farm, do you mean? And now you feel that because of this wicked rumour you can't apply for it? But that's ridiculous."

"It isn't because of the rumour," he said unhappily. "I can disregard that, knowing there's not a grain of truth in it and believing it was started out of jealousy. What's shattered my dreams is something quite different. I—I'm not even sure I can tell you about it."

"But if it . . . That is, you did lead me to suppose your plans concerned me in some way."

"Yes, you're right, you've a right to know. Just let me pen these sheep and then . . ."

"I'll help you. Do you want the gate to the pound opened?"

"Yes, if you would, please." He smiled, the anxiety temporarily banished from his face. "You've not forgotten moorland ways, have you?"

"I should hope not," she said indignantly, and set off up a track which would take her around the flock and down ahead of them to the pound on the valley bottom.

When the sheep were penned, Alan dismounted and Jennifer followed suit. He stood scuffing at a root of ling for a few minutes, while she waited in an expectant silence. At last he asked, "Do you still believe in witchcraft, Jenny?"

Surprised, she said, "To a certain extent. I know there are men and women who can foretell events, and so-called white witches who can cure warts and . . ."

"I didn't mean white witches, but black ones."

A little shiver ran down Jennifer's spine. "What are you getting at?"

"Promise you won't say a word to anyone if I tell you?"

"I promise."

"My mother knew how much I wanted the chance of taking over Stadden when Ben died," Alan said, with some reluctance. "She said she'd like to help me if she could."

"Naturally she would. Anything that *you* want . . . I'm sorry, go on."

"When I asked her how she thought she could help, she answered in a very strange manner, 'There *are* ways.' "

"There was nothing sinister in that, surely?"

"I didn't think so at the time, but the next morning I saw her walking up towards Gibbet Tor."

"What of it?" she asked, as he paused. "She'd probably gone to collect whortleberries or lichen for dyeing purposes. There's plenty of both up there."

"She didn't go to gather anything, Jenny. I followed her."

She looked at him incredulously. "You . . .? Alan, what *are* you trying to tell me?"

"Mother was making for Hannah Sculpher's cottage. *Cottage,*" he repeated scornfully. " 'Tis no more than a hovel, I'd not house a pig in it. But you must know what Hannah's reputation is."

"That she's a black witch?"

"Yes," he said. "Now do you see? It was the following day when I found Ben Cobbledick, dead at the foot of the ladder."

Jennifer drew in her breath and held it, then let it out again slowly. "You can't really think . . . Oh, Alan, it's too silly and far-fetched. To imagine that your mother would ask old Hannah Sculpher to make an effigy of poor Ben and stick pins into it . . ."

"She'd not have done that," he said gravely. "She'd have made an effigy, for sure, and then broken its neck if that's how . . ."

"Alan, stop it! You *can't* believe this! You *mustn't!*"

He took hold of her shoulders and turned her to face him. "Look me in the eyes and tell me that you don't believe it, that you haven't the slightest doubt, the least grain of suspicion . . ."

"Of course I haven't," she said, much too quickly. "Admittedly your mother is—is not like most of the other farmers' wives I know and she has a certain reserve and—and strangeness which I've always put down to . . ."

"The likelihood of gipsy blood?"

"Yes, but even so, she'd never do what you suggest, surely?" When he did not reply, she asked again, "Surely you don't really think . . . ?"

He released her and turned away. "The thought first came to me when you'd gone to fetch the doctor. It's been in my mind ever since. I can't get rid of it, Jenny, and—and it's spoiled everything. I couldn't take Ben's farm now, suspecting that my own mother . . ." He buried his face in his hands.

Jennifer put a hand on his arm. "Alan, please. You mustn't upset yourself like this. Why don't you question your mother and then you'll probably find that she just wanted to have a chat with old

Hannah about some remedy to cure a broody hen or . . ."

"If that were the case, she'd have gone to a white witch, wouldn't she, not a black one?"

His face and voice were so filled with despair that she did not know what to say. And now, she realized with dismay, the seed of suspicion was germinating in her own mind. She had not lived on Dartmoor for seventeen of her nineteen years without being aware of strange happenings which could not be explained by rational means. There was the atmosphere surrounding the standing stones, for instance, near where the American had been thrown from his horse. There were inexplicable eerie sounds which came at night from the disused tin mines. There was Dewer and his wish hounds, and ghostly monks who trod the Lych Way, the path of the dead . . .

She shivered involuntarily. Then she realized Alan had been watching her closely.

"You see?" he said bleakly. "You're not certain that it couldn't have happened. Because I can't be sure, there never could be any peace for me if I took Stadden. I'd always have the feeling I'd acquired it because of some—some . . ." He shook his head, his face grim. "No, I can't say the word, not about my own mother. But it's there in my mind, nagging away, all the time. And I ought not to have told you, that's for sure."

But he *had* told her, and because she could never

be presented with a problem, her own or anyone else's, without immediately trying to find a way to solve it, she decided against going back with him to Edgecombe Farm for tea and instead made the excuse that she had work to do for her father. But although she started out homewards, once out of Alan's sight she set the mare's head towards the track which led steeply up out of the valley and towards Gibbet Tor.

Jennifer had never actually had any conversation with Hannah Sculpher. Once or twice, seeing her on the moor, she had spoken a greeting, only to be met with a hard stare from Hannah's extraordinarily dark eyes. The old woman certainly had the appearance of a witch, with her hooked nose and jutting chin, but Jennifer's mother had dismissed the idea, saying she was just a poor mazed creature who chose to live like a recluse, existing on berries, rabbits which had escaped from the warren, an occasional lamb killed by a fox and any wild birds she could trap or snare. Peat and furze provided her fireing and a stream ran just below the old tinner's blowing-house which she had taken over as her home and which was sheltered from the wind which blew off Gibbet Tor by a small wood of stunted oaks, reputed locally to be haunted.

Once, in childhood, Mollie had dared Jennifer to go up there alone and ask the "black witch" to cast a spell over the village bully. Always ready to accept a challenge, Jennifer had set off bravely enough but when she saw Hannah, dressed as usual in a strange collection of tattered black garments, sitting on a boulder and stirring some horrible smelling concoction in a black pan hanging from a tripod of sticks over a smoky fire, her courage had failed her.

Now she was older and more sensible. At least, she hoped so. And she had Bracken for company. But as she rode down beside the wood, the mare began to show signs of nervousness. Jennifer patted her neck and spoke reassuringly, glad to hear her own voice in this strange, silent place. Reining in within a few yards of the hovel, she called, "Mistress Sculpher, are you there?"

Her only reply was the croak of a raven which flew up from the edge of the wood.

As Bracken shied, Jennifer said sharply, "Don't be stupid, it's only a bird," and was aware that she was trying to reassure herself as well as the mount, for a raven was regarded as a bird of ill omen.

Bracken began to play her up, so she dismounted and tethered the pony firmly to a stout branch. Then, grasping her whip, she went towards the building and called again. Still getting no response, she pushed open the rickety door and looked inside. The room, dark and smelling of damp, was empty. On the beaten earth floor were some bare bones and a pitcher of water on the surface of which dead flies floated. There was a pile of bracken in one corner, presumably used as a bed, a three-legged stool, a stump of candle on a tin plate. The whole appear-

ance was almost as primitive as that of the prehistoric hut circles at Grimspound.

With a return of the panic she had felt as a child,
Jennifer retreated hastily and closed the door. She
tried to take a grip on herself. If Hannah Sculpher
was not even here, what was there to be afraid of?
And even if she were, what possible harm could
she do to a strong, healthy young woman who could
mount her pony and ride away within minutes?
Yet there were so many tales told about the old
crone, of humans being ill-wished, animals being
over-looked so that they sickened and died.

"Oh, don't be so silly!" Jennifer chided herself
aloud. "You've just been telling Alan not to be so
foolish as to believe this kind of nonsense and now
you're behaving just as stupidly."

She was about to turn when she thought she saw
something moving in the wood. She called, "Is anybody there? Mistress Sculpher, is that you?"

Her mare, still nervous, shied at the sound of her
voice, and the only answer she had was the grating
of a horseshoe against a granite boulder. Either she
had been mistaken or the old crone did not want to
be seen. Yet, with a strange sensation of being
driven into action against her will, she moved to the
edge of the wood and peered into its shadowy in-
terior. There *was* something there. It looked like a
piece of black material, stirred by a sudden breeze.

Jennifer's heart was beating fast. Her hands were
cold and clammy. She wanted to turn and run, to

mount Bracken and ride away as quickly as she could, but she was still held by the odd feeling of compulsion. Quietly, holding her breath, she crept forward, bending nearly double beneath the lichen-covered branches of the stunted oaks. Ahead of her the oaks thinned but a bigger tree had found a foothold for its roots down amongst a tumble of boulders. One of the stones had a patch of moss scraped away, as if someone or something had scrambled on to it. Jennifer looked upwards.

She screamed then, and went on screaming, while cold sweat broke out all over her body. Then she turned and scrambled recklessly back the way she had come, risking broken bones as she sought to escape as fast as she could from this horrible place and what she had seen.

Her hands were trembling so violently that it was several moments before she could untether Bracken. Then she flung herself on to the mare's back and galloped wildly down the hill. At the bottom she reined in, slid from the saddle and, her legs buckling beneath her, fell headlong amongst the heather. She lay there, face downwards, clutching at the tough stalks, sobbing and retching and crying out, in a voice scarcely recognizable as her own, "*No!* Oh, *no!* Oh, God, don't let it be true!"

At last she became aware of another voice, a man's, close beside her. It was a few moments before she could control herself enough to turn over and sit up. Darrell Meares was on his knees beside her, regarding her with the greatest concern in his grey eyes. He put his arm about her shoulders.

"Miss Haslam, what's happened? I heard screaming, and then saw you galloping down the hill. What is it? Tell me."

"I—I . . ." But she could not tell him. She could only press her hands to her mouth for fear she would start retching again.

He took out his handkerchief and wiped her face. Then he urged gently, "Try to tell me. Are you hurt?"

She shook her head, still not trusting herself to speak.

"All right," he said. "Just take your time."

His arms about her shoulders, his deep, calm voice, were immensely reassuring. Fear and horror had driven out all other thoughts so that she leaned against him, clutching at his sleeve, while she tried desperately to regain control of herself.

He said, "I'm going to take you home, Miss Haslam. Put your arm round my neck and I'll . . ."

"No. No, please, you must . . ." She took a deep breath and concentrated on every word. "I want you to—to go up there to the little wood behind Hannah Sculpher's cottage . . ."

"I'm not going to anybody's cottage," he broke in, "not until I've taken you home."

"You *must*." In her desperation she shook his arm. "*Please*. I must know."

"Must know what?"

"If—if what I saw was true, that I didn't imagine it."

"What *did* you see?" He bent to look into her face. "Something that frightened you, made you scream?"

"Yes. Only . . . It was so—so horrible that I didn't look properly and I may have imagined . . . Please go and look, go now, at once."

"I can't leave you . . ."

"I'll be all right. I'll just wait here until you come back."

"If that is really what you want."

She nodded vehemently. Her strength was returning now although she was trembling. She said, "If you would just bring Bracken over to me, she'll keep me company."

"Bracken?" he repeated doubtfully.

"My pony. She's the same colour, you see."

He rose and led the mare quietly to her and put the reins into her hand. Then he pulled a silver flask from his pocket and offered it to her. She shook her head but he insisted.

"Take a little. That's an order."

She looked up at him. He seemed very tall and commanding in his light coloured breeches and green coat, his beaver hat at an angle on his fair hair.

"Very well," she said obediently, and took a few sips of brandy.

She began to feel better then, and when he urged

her to drink some more, she did so without argument.

"That's good," he said, "the colour's coming back to your cheeks. Now, what is it you want me to look for?"

"I—don't want to tell you. I'd just like you to go into the wood. You'll have to bend low because of the branches, and after a bit you'll find a little clearing and a big tree and there . . . Go now, please, and then come back and tell me . . . Pray God you can tell me I was mistaken."

She watched him as he mounted the chestnut and rode quickly off up the hill. She drank a little more brandy and then found a boulder to lean against. She began talking to Bracken, thankful to hear her voice sounding almost normal, although a bit shaky and slightly slurred. She wondered if she was becoming tipsy. Perhaps it would be as well if she were, if Darrell Meares should confirm what she had seen. Despite the doubt she had expressed to him, she had none in her own mind. And even worse than what she had seen was its implication. For, surely, there could be only one explanation. Hannah Sculpher, having brought about Ben Cobbledick's death by witchcraft, had been overcome by remorse and hanged herself in the little wood behind her tumbledown cottage. And if that *were* true, then it must follow that Alan had been right in his suspicion about his mother's part in the affair.

Jennifer tipped up the flask and drained the last

drop of brandy. The tors on the other side of the valley began to waver. Her own voice, talking nonsense to Bracken, sounded far away. She closed her eyes but the world was still unsteady and her head fell forward. She began to hiccup gently and then to giggle. When she heard the thud of hooves and Bracken's welcoming whinny, she opened her eyes and saw two men, both riding chestnut horses, or so it seemed to her. And when the American knelt beside her once again and started to speak, she could not understand a single word of what he was saying.

"The very idea!"

The voice was Mrs Westcott's, sharp with disapproval. Jennifer opened her eyes and found that she was in her own room, lying on her bed. How she came to be there she had no idea and her head was too muzzy to try to work it out. Vaguely she remembered being lifted up, then clutching a horse's mane that was not Bracken's and thinking how far she was above the ground. The ground itself would not stay still and the tors kept coming nearer and then receding and there was a man's voice but she could not take in what he was saying.

"What—what happened?" she asked the housekeeper dazedly.

"You may well ask! The very idea of drinking a whole flask of brandy! If that's the kind of behaviour you were taught in London, then 'tis a great pity your father ever allowed you to go. Now come along, eat these biscuits. At least that will give the drink something to work on."

"I—don't want . . ."

" 'Tis not what you want, my girl, but what's good for you."

Although it was difficult to get Mrs Westcott's face into focus, Jennifer could see it was no use to argue. Obediently she nibbled a few biscuits. She did not remember ever feeling so dreadful, and the housekeeper's carping voice, going on and on, made her head ache.

"I never thought to see anything so disgraceful in this house. To come riding home, with a man's arms around you and him a 'foreigner' at that, and so drunk you could not even stand and . . ."

"Oh, do stop, *please*," Jennifer pleaded. "If you only knew . . ."

"Knew what? I suppose you'm thinking up some excuse . . ."

To Jennifer's relief there was a tap on the door and her father came in.

"My dear child, what a terrible thing to have happened! Mr Meares has just been telling me . . ."

Mrs Westcott looked disconcerted, then returned to the attack. "You could trust *that* fine gentleman to think up some story."

"Mrs Westcott, will you please leave us," Professor Haslam said, in a tone of unusual firmness. "Jennifer has been though a most distressing experience. The last thing she needs, or deserves, is to be subjected to reproof."

"I was only trying to do my duty, seeing Miss Jenny has no mother . . . Oh, very well." Clearly affronted, the housekeeper stalked from the room.

Jennifer began to giggle, then took a hold on herself. "Papa, I'm sorry. I—I made a fool of myself, but . . ."

"It's all right, my dear." Her father sat beside the bed and took hold of her hand. "Do you feel able to talk?"

"Yes. To you, at any rate."

"Then tell me first, what were you doing up at Hannah Sculpher's cottage?"

She closed her eyes, knowing that she must think out carefully what she said, but it was so difficult to concentrate. "I had been to see Mollie and then Alan, and—and I helped him gather in some sheep and then it seemed a good idea to ride home by Gibbet Tor."

"But that is two miles out of your way."

"I know, but . . . Bracken was still fresh and . . ." She gave up and lay back. "Anyway, that's what I did."

"Even so, my dear, that doesn't account for . . ."

"Papa, must you question me now? My head . . ."

He patted her hand. "I'll leave you to rest a while. Whatever your reason for going there, I am very thankful that Mr Meares was exercising his horse in that direction and came upon you."

"Yes, so am I," she said, then added in a surprised voice, "He was very kind and understanding. I wouldn't have expected that."

"I cannot imagine why. Any gentleman, finding a young girl in distress, alone on the moor . . ."

"I have declared war on him," she said, and it sounded so foolish that she wanted to laugh, but managed to stop herself from doing so.

"I suppose you know what you are talking about," her father said, rising, "but I am completely at a loss. At your first meeting with Mr Meares, by your own account you made some extremely regrettable remarks but I assumed that your letter of apology would have been accepted and Mr Meares, who I cannot imagine to be a gentleman to bear any resentment . . ."

"You don't know him, Papa, and you certainly *can't* imagine . . ." She put a hand to her head. It was all too difficult. In any case, there was something much more important hammering at her mind if only she could think what it was.

"I will leave you now," her father said, making for the door.

It was as he reached it that her mind suddenly cleared. "Papa, wait, please. There's something I must know. Did Mr Meares say . . . that is, did he find . . . ?" She sat up. To her relief, the room had steadied and her voice sounded almost normal. "Papa, I *must* know if I imagined what I saw in that wood."

"It depends on what you think you saw," her father said guardedly.

"It looked like a—a bundle of black rags hanging from a branch, but I think—I am sure, it was Mistress Sculpher."

"You did not imagine it," her father answered gravely. "Mr Meares is now on his way to inform Mr Venner."

"Because he is a magistrate—Mr Venner, I mean?"

"Yes. It seemed the best plan."

"Did he—Mr Meares—think it was—murder, then?"

"No, no. It seemed to him clear that the poor soul had done away with herself—some weeks ago, it would appear. Now try and put it from your mind."

"No, not yet, Papa, please don't go, not yet." Jennifer got off the bed, clutching at a chair for support, then crossed to her washstand and poured water from the jug into the basin and splashed it over her face. Then she pressed a wet flannel to her forehead. When she turned back to her father, she found him regarding her anxiously.

"Papa, will you repeat what you said?" she asked.

"About what?"

"About Hannah Sculpher. You said—at least, I thought you did but my head is still not very clear, some weeks ago . . ."

"Yes, that is so. She must have been hanging

there, without anyone finding her, for some considerable time, so Mr Meares conjectured. It is very dreadful to realize that people can be left . . . But then, it was how she chose to live, to be left to her own devices, and those devices were not always . . . But she is dead now, God rest her soul and you must try to forget . . ."

"I can't do that, not yet, Papa, not until I've told Alan . . ."

"What has Alan to do with this?"

"I can't explain, but I must see him. Perhaps if I had something to eat, as Mrs Westcott suggested, then I could ride . . ."

"My dear child, you are not riding anywhere, *or* leaving this house again today. For one thing, you are not fit to do so, and for another, it is extremely likely that Mr Venner will be coming here to question you. That, I fear, will be distressing for you, but . . ."

"Then at least let me send Alan a message. Zebedee could take a note."

"Why this insistence?"

"Because Alan . . ." Hastily she thought up an answer that was at least similar to the truth. "He had been making enquiries, about Hannah Sculpher. He—he hadn't seen her about for some time, and so I suppose . . ." Her voice tailed off as she saw her father's expression.

"Jennifer, you have never been very good at

evasion. If you will just tell me that neither you nor Alan has done anything in this affair of which you are ashamed, then I will accept your assurance and ask no more questions."

"I can assure you of that, Papa, truly. And you will allow me to send a note?"

"Certainly, if it will set your mind at rest."

He brought her pen and paper and after a little thought she wrote a note which she hoped would completely reassure Alan without giving too much away should it fall into his mother's hands.

Dear Alan, she wrote. *You can forget what we talked about after we'd penned the sheep. The person we mentioned is dead. It was her own neck she broke, some weeks ago. I expect you will hear more about it soon. Jenny.*

Alan and Darrell arrived at Lidden Barton simultaneously that evening. Alan knew at once who Darrell was, for he had seen him riding about the moor, but to the American Alan was just another moorland farmer, although better dressed than most, and better educated, too.

"Good evening," Alan said affably. "You are calling on Professor Haslam, I expect. I believe you share his interest in antiquities."

"My interest at present is in *Miss* Haslam," Darrell said, hitching his horse's reins to the gate-post.

"Oh? I didn't know you'd even met her."

"Why should you know, Mr . . . ?"

"Vicary. Alan Vicary's my name. I'm a friend of Jennifer's, have been since we were children. I was one of Professor Haslam's pupils, before I went to grammar school. That's a beautiful animal." He patted the chestnut's arched neck. "Don't you find it a bit too highly bred, though? I believe you took a toss, trying to force it past a row of standing stones up by . . . ?"

"Who told you about that?" Darrell asked sharply.

Surprised at the angry flush spreading over the older man's face, Alan said mildly, "Someone in Wellsworthy. It's nothing to be ashamed of. A creature like this would be extra sensitive and I dare say that as a stranger you didn't know about such things."

"What *things,* Mr Vicary?" Darrell asked coldly.

"Places with strange atmospheres. Animals are very aware of . . ."

"I'm afraid I cannot accept credence in such beliefs. Naturally, people brought up in such primitive surroundings and who have never left Dartmoor . . ."

"Professor Haslam wasn't brought up here," Alan broke in, "but he believes in—certain inexplicable phenomena, I think he'd call it. Perhaps in America it's different, perhaps over there you have an answer to all mysteries."

Darrell took a step forward. "Are you being sarcastic?"

"No more than you are," Alan answered equably. "Excuse me, Jenny'll be expecting me."

He went quickly up the steps and knocked on the door. He had heard a great deal about this American who had put so many people's backs up but neither he nor any of his family had any personal grudge against Darrell Meares and he had no wish to start a quarrel. The incident of the American being thrown from his horse had been related to him by Mollie. The fact that Jennifer herself had not told him, Alan had put down to their having so many other things to talk about.

Darrell came swiftly up the steps to stand beside Alan. "Miss Haslam, I feel sure, will also be expecting *me*." He drew himself up to his full height, topping Alan by a few inches.

When the door was opened by Mrs Westcott, Alan, determined to get in first, said, "Jenny wrote me a note. She'll be wanting to see me."

"*I* came to enquire if Miss Haslam has recovered from her unfortunate experience." Darrell's drawl was very pronounced.

The housekeeper shrugged and stood aside. "You'd best both come in, and I'll see . . . Oh, here is Miss Jenny."

Jennifer, coming down the stairs, looked taken aback to see the two men standing below. As they both stepped forward, Professor Haslam emerged from his study. He looked over the top of his spectacles at Alan, seeming momentarily to have difficulty in placing him, then nodded affably and turned to Darrell.

"Ah, Mr Meares, good evening. That matter of the kistvaen up near Hen Tor that we were discussing . . . I've discovered . . . But come inside, come into my study."

Disconcerted, Darrell tried to demur. "I came, sir, actually to . . ."

"Borrow the book I mentioned? Yes, of course you may. I'm sure Jennifer and Alan will excuse us."

He took hold of Darrell's arm and ushered him into the study. Jennifer could scarcely contain her laughter and Alan was delighted at her father's intervention. Following her into the parlour, he said, "I don't wonder that American puts people's backs up. He's an arrogant fellow."

"Yes, he can be, but there *is* another side, as I discovered this afternoon. Oh, I have so much to tell you!"

They sat together in the window seat while she explained what lay behind the cryptic note she had sent him.

"So you see, you were absolutely wrong," she declared when she came to the end of the story. "Ben Cobbledick's death was an accident, pure and simple, and neither you nor your mother was in any way involved or to blame. Mr Venner confirmed what Mr Meares had said, that poor old Hannah Sculpher had been dead for some weeks. Now I think we should forget the whole affair. I certainly want to do so, it was so dreadful."

Alan remained silent, staring down at the river which gleamed faintly between the beeches just below the house. The valley was growing dark now that the sun had gone down behind the opposite hill. Then he turned to smile at her and, taking hold of her hand, squeezed it warmly.

"It's a tremendous relief. But, Jenny, what made you go up to Hannah's cottage?"

"I wanted to see if I could find out from her . . ."

"You would have confronted her, knowing her reputation?"

"I didn't think she could do me any harm. Anyway, why should she want to? I admit I was nervous, though, and I didn't *want* to go."

"But you *did,* for my sake?"

She nodded, her face very serious in the fading light. "You were so worried and unhappy, and you'd been so kind, Alan, meeting me at Moreton, giving me Bracken, taking the trouble to break her in and school her to a side-saddle. I saw the chance to do something for you, in return."

He was grateful, there was no doubt about that, but at the same time he could not help a slight feeling of disappointment. It sounded in his voice as he said, "It was good of you, Jenny, but—but had it nothing to do with what I told you about my plans for Ben's place? I mean, since you knew I hoped they would involve you as well . . ."

Jennifer withdrew her hand and rose, turning slightly away from him. "I've had a great shock today, Alan. I don't think now is the right time . . ."

Contrite, he said at once, "I'm sorry, I'm being selfish. You must have gone through a terrible time and I'm so grateful to you. I'll go now, if you like."

She nodded, smiling at him. "If you don't mind. I *am* tired."

He was almost at the door when a thought struck him. Turning back, he said, "I gather that this afternoon wasn't the first time you've met Mr Meares. Mollie told me about the incident when you saw him thrown from his horse but I didn't know you'd actually spoken to him."

She hesitated, and bent to rearrange a cushion on the window-seat. Her voice sounded oddly strained as she said, "I didn't, not at that time. But, yes, I had met him. On both occasions he—he made me very angry. I'll tell you more when—when I'm not so tired."

"All right," he said, trying to hide the hurt he was feeling, as well as surprise. "Sleep well, Jenny, and my thanks again, for what you did for me."

He was opening the gate into the rough meadow which ran alongside the river when he glanced up and saw that the lamps had been lit in the parlour. Jennifer was silhouetted against their soft glow. He saw her move forward. The next moment the American was standing close beside her, holding her hands, smiling down at her.

Alan was shocked by the intensity of his reaction. He clanged the gate shut, flung himself across the saddle and was urging his pony into a gallop before he had even got his feet in the stirrups. For the first time in his life he vented his own outraged feelings upon an animal, and it was only the sure-footedness of the pony that saved them both from disaster as he rode recklessly amongst boulders and twisted heather roots, in the gathering darkness of the valley between the steep, cold hills.

Chapter Four

Jennifer and her father had been invited to dinner at Heronslea. Jennifer's inclination had been to decline. However kindly Darrell Meares had behaved to her, it did not alter the fact that he had brought hardship to people she loved or had known all her life. To accept hospitality at Heronslea was to enter the house of the enemy. On the other hand, it might prove a good move on her part. Not every fight was won by bloodshed or in anger. Particularly for a woman, there were the more subtle weapons of persuasion, flattery, cajolery. Although she preferred more forthright methods, what mattered was that she should obtain justice for her friends.

The selection of the dress she would wear took her some time but she eventually decided on one of gold taffeta with a flounced skirt and a low neckline edged with Honiton lace. She gave her hair a good brushing and lengthened her ringlets and then draped a Paisley shawl about her shoulders. She was gratified by the admiration in Mrs Westcott's eyes and wondered what effect her "London appearance" would have had on Alan.

Darrell had offered to send his carriage to fetch them. Twenty minutes before it was due, Jennifer found her father still in his study, happily immersed in a list of chapter headings for his new book. She shooed him up to his bedroom where she had laid out his evening clothes, then made sure he combed his hair and changed his shoes. When he was finally ready, she tucked her arm in his so that he should not escape.

"Papa, have you ever been inside Mr Meares' house?" she asked.

"No. I've been no further than the door. It has been constructed on the lines of a colonial mansion, I believe."

"It is certainly imposing. But then, that is what one would expect of him."

"You sound disapproving, my dear. Why shouldn't a gentleman build himself an imposing residence if he so wishes?"

"No reason at all. It's just that it makes it doubly hard, I think, for the people whose lives he has made more difficult."

"Ah, you are banner-waving again. Your aunt wrote me, I seem to recall, that in London you developed what she described as 'some dangerously radical ideas.' "

"Just because I wanted to do something to relieve the terrible conditions . . ."

"My dear, you cannot transform the world."

"I might be able to transform Mr Meares, though," she said, less seriously.

"Oh dear," her father murmured, running a hand through his hair. "I fear I may be in for a most disturbing evening. I would much prefer to remain at home and . . ."

"It's too late, Papa. I can hear the carriage arriving."

Jennifer's first impression, as they reached Heronslea, was that the house had been built the wrong way round. She supposed it faced east in order to obtain the best view, but she would as soon have sunlight as a view, and the front would entrap the sun's rays for only a short while each morning. She had often thought it strange that so few people noticed which way a house faced. To a farmer, his home was simply somewhere to eat and be comfortable in, after his day's work in the open. His wife spent most of her time in yard or kitchen. In London, where families lived mostly indoors, the darkness of the rooms had made an immediate, and unfavourable, impression on Jennifer. It seemed to her now especially odd that a man used to the hot sun of Carolina should not have planned to take advantage of every moment of the more fitful sunshine of Dartmoor.

Certainly it was one of the most elegant houses

she had ever seen. The sash windows were evenly spaced, balancing the long roof of blue slates, and the entrance porch, reached by a flight of six steps, was supported on white pillars. The whole building could not have been more in contrast to the original, half-finished, Heronslea, which had incorporated Gothic turrets and tiny, latticed windows overhung with thatch.

As they went up the steps, her father remarked, "It appears as if *this* house will be completed but I doubt if it will have any more permanence than the previous one."

"Why not, Papa?" Jennifer asked in surprise. "Surely Mr Meares intends to remain here?"

"I dare say he does, for the present. He has yet to experience a winter on the moor."

"Did he not stay at the Duchy Hotel in Princetown last winter while the building was in its early stages?"

"Only while the weather was good. As soon as it turned colder, he moved down to Torquay. I like this young American but I fear he has rather more money than sense. He . . . Oh, good gracious! I had quite forgotten."

Jennifer, who had been looking at the view down the valley, turned to see what had startled her father. She found that the door had been silently opened. A huge Negro in an immaculate white suit, was bowing and inviting them inside.

As Jennifer stepped over the threshold, she felt

as if she were entering another world. It was not only the presence of the coloured butler but also the whole appearance of the big hall. The floor was of black and white chequered tiles and a wide staircase swept up in a graceful curve to a landing which ran right round the house, giving a feeling of drama and spaciousness.

The butler took her cloak and her father's coat, and then the American was greeting them, bowing over her hand, holding it a little longer than was necessary. Once again, noticing how extremely handsome he looked in his evening clothes, experiencing a little tremor of excitement as her fingers were clasped in his, she wished the enemy did not have this disturbing effect on her.

He spent half an hour showing them round the house, explaining the architecture, talking of future plans. She noticed how frequently he referred to his previous home in South Carolina or mentioned that some feature was copied from a house on a neighbouring plantation. Again she wondered, as did everyone else except her father who would not trouble himself with such questions, why the American had left his own land and come here, to settle in such a totally different environment.

It was during dinner that she found an opportunity to ask him. He had been telling her father of the stone rows he had visited at Carnac in Brittany, comparing them with the ones on Dartmoor.

"Is that what brought you here in the first place?" she asked, "to look at the antiquities?"

"Oh, no. I had been travelling around England and came west to visit Bristol where my family originated. Then I decided to go to Plymouth and have a look at the place from where the Pilgrim Fathers eventually set sail in the Mayflower to cross the Atlantic. While in Plymouth I heard about the prison on the moor where a number of my country-men joined the French as prisoners-of-war. And so I arrived on Dartmoor."

"And saw it as a wilderness to be conquered?"

"Yes," he answered, sounding surprised. "But how did you . . . ?"

"You are not the first. There have been other men who have tried, and failed."

"*I* shall not fail," he declared somewhat arro-gantly. "I am not, for instance, attempting the im-possible, such as planning to grow vast acres of corn and wheat."

"You are attempting flax and hemp, though, I believe."

"On a small scale, yes. But as you must have seen, it is mostly trees."

"Afforestation was tried at Tor Royal but it was not successful."

"That was because it was not done properly."

"And you will do it properly?" Jennifer suggested with some asperity.

"I hope so. In any case, I am not without money,

Miss Haslam, I can afford to make a few mistakes."

"How very gratifying for you. The men who farm small holdings on Dartmoor are not so fortunate. It is all they can do to make ends meet."

"That is because they *are* small—in their thinking as well as their acreage."

She asked indignantly, "What chance has a moorman . . . ?"

"As much chance—more, in fact,—as my forebears and hundreds of immigrants had when they first reached the shores of America, with no assets except their own courage and determination."

For a moment she was taken aback. Then she saw the answer to that argument. "But there was land there for the taking—a whole continent open to them—except, of course, that they had to steal it from the Indians just as you are . . ."

"Stealing land from the commoners? You still persist in that idea, despite my assurance that I have a legal document . . ."

"Which the Duchy should not have granted you. They are contravening the rights of copyhold and venville which go back hundreds of years."

"Then why is not evidence of these rights produced?"

"Because they have been taken for granted, or—or," she went on uncertainly, seeing his scornful expression, "in some cases the documents may have been lost."

"Then the commoners have been extremely careless, have they not? And I can scarcely be blamed for that."

At that moment, Professor Haslam, whose mind had been so preoccupied that he had remained oblivious to the exchange taking place between his daughter and their host, turned to Darrell.

"Regarding the relative positions of the standing stones at Carnac, I should like to discuss with you my theory that the position of the sun at certain times of the days plays a far more significant part in their alignment than people have hitherto appreciated."

"Certainly, sir, but I would suggest that Miss Haslam . . ."

"Oh, Jennifer won't mind, will you, my dear?"

"Of course not, Papa," she answered, thankful for the change of subject. Despite her resolution to remain calm, she had once again been so provoked by the American's attitude that she had been on the point of losing her temper.

When the meal was over and they went into the drawing-room, Darrell led the professor to a side table on which were several books.

"Perhaps you would like to browse through these," he suggested, "while I show your daughter some tapestries I bought in Plymouth recently."

The tapestries lay over the back of a sofa. Standing beside Jennifer while she admired them, he asked, "You are skilled in needlework, Miss Haslam?"

"Not this kind of needlework. Oh, I can mend and darn and . . . That shocks you, I suppose," she said, seeing his expression. "Doubtless you are accustomed to ladies who leave such tasks to their servants, or employ a seamstress. But we live practical lives up here on the moor, from necessity if not always from choice."

"Does that mean you would not choose . . . ?"

"To live here? Oh, indeed I would. Why *you* should do so remains still a mystery."

"But I mentioned during dinner . . ."

"That you saw the moor as virgin country to be exploited? Yes, so you did. Even so, there must surely be large tracts of far more suitable land in America. Papa thinks you will find it very cold here in winter."

"Possibly. In that case, I shall move elsewhere."

"You mean . . . ?" Strangely, she felt both hope and regret.

"I mean, during the bad weather. I am sorry to disappoint you, Miss Haslam, but you will not get rid of me as easily as that."

"What makes you think . . . ?"

"You have made it very obvious that you wish me a thousand miles away—three thousand, in fact, on the other side of the Atlantic."

She thought, if I am careful, I could turn this moment to some good effect. Smiling up at him, she said, "That is not true, Mr Meares. I should be delighted to have you as a neighbour, if only . . ."

"If only I would go to the Duchy's agent and say, 'I have made a mistake and so have you. In fact, we have committed a criminal act and appropriated land which is not ours by right but belongs to a handful of peasants who . . .' "

He caught himself up but it was too late. "I'm sorry," he said quickly, "That was . . ."

"Why apologize for a word which came so naturally to you? It had already occurred to me, and I see now that I was right, that you would regard such people as the graziers who have rights over the land you have enclosed, and the warrener who is the father of one of my closest friends, as on a par with the negroes on your plantation, of no account, to be made use of, or disposed of, according to your whim."

She thought, now *I* have gone too far. I meant to stay calm and try to win him over. Instead, I have again allowed his overbearing attitude to anger me. That he was angry, too, there was no doubt. His face was set, the corners of his mouth pulled in, his eyes hard. In the silence, Jennifer heard her father exclaiming quietly and with pleasure over the books. She thought, I shall have to apologize, at once, before the evening is ruined.

She said quietly, "I am sorry. I should not have spoken so rudely when I am a guest in your house."

"What difference does that make? If your feelings are so roused by my conduct, why allow some foolish convention to stop you from expressing them?"

"It was discourteous."

"Oh, come now, Miss Haslam, it is a little late to be concerned on that score. I scarcely think our conduct towards one another—except, perhaps, yesterday . . ."

"When you were so kind," she put in quickly, "and I—disgraced myself."

"By taking too much brandy? Perhaps I should try to persuade you to do the same now. Perhaps you need to be a little—tipsy, before you are prepared to call a truce. Do not look so cross, I am only teasing you."

Perplexed, she studied his face. She found it impossible to decide whether he was merely amused or whether, behind the easy manner which had so swiftly followed his anger, he was contemptuous of her. After all, what must she appear to him? A young woman too outspoken to be a lady, in her aunt's sense of the word, and yet too cultured, thanks to her father, to be just a country girl. And again she recalled what Mollie had said to her on her first morning back.

"You don't really belong in any one world, like other people. It's not that simple for you, Jenny."

It certainly was not simple at this moment. Foolishly she had imagined that by using a few feminine wiles, she could bring this young American round to her point of view, even persuade him to change his mind and make some concessions. Now she saw that she was up against a man who was convinced that everything he did was right and whose arrogance, she suspected, would not even let him listen to anyone else's point of view. A man moreover, whose life had been easy from the beginning, and who meant to keep it so. The battle was lost before it was even begun. What chance had she of persuading a man of wealth and property, used to being obeyed without question by everyone not of his own class, to change his views? If he had no sense of justice, or compassion . . .

There, surely, was the core of the matter. He had shown *her* kindness, certainly, but she was a young and not unattractive woman and he had been given the opportunity to play Sir Galahad, which few men could resist. But to those he considered his inferiors, there would never be any such consideration. Had she not already had evidence of how hard and callous he could be, the day he chased poor Zebedee?

He had left her side and gone to a table on which the butler had placed a silver tray with glasses and decanters. Incensed by what she suspected he was about to do, she said hotly, "You were not teasing, were you? You intend to try and make me . . ."

"You are quite mistaken," he said coolly. "I do not so flatter myself as to imagine that I could make you do anything you did not wish. I was about to pour some brandy for your father."

Her fan hung from a ribbon around her wrist. It was all she could do to restrain herself from striking him with it. Instead, she turned abruptly away and made a pretence of examining the tapestries more closely. The colours blurred as, inexplicably, her eyes filled with tears. She had never felt so humiliated, never been reduced to tears of mortification by any man. She longed to be with Alan, dear, uncomplicated Alan, who would never dream of treating her as if she were an unruly child, who had to be humoured, which seemed to her what Darrell Meares was doing at present.

Her father said, "How very kind of you, Mr Meares, to look out these books for me. I must confess, I usually try to avoid social occasions, and I decline most invitations these days unless they are connected with my work, but I am greatly enjoying this evening."

"I am so glad," Darrell said, with a slight bow. "I could only wish your daughter felt the same."

"Jennifer? Oh, she always enjoys herself. Except, at times in London, I believe. I should have realized, I suppose, that town life would not appeal to her, Dartmoor being her landscape of the heart. We all have them, of course. Yours, I dare say, would be South Carolina."

"*No!*"

The word was like the crack of a whip, making Jennifer swing round in surprise.

Her father blinked behind his spectacles. "I am

sorry if I inadvertently . . . That is to say, I imagined that South Carolina, being your former home . . ."

"I should prefer not to talk of it," Darrell said, and pouring himself a stiff brandy, drank it so quickly it caught his breath.

Watching him, Jennifer experienced a quick change of mood. His reaction seemed to her to suggest that he was, after all, vulnerable. There was a chink in the armour, if only she could discover it.

Keeping her voice carefully casual, she asked, "Was that your real reason for staying on Dartmoor, Mr Meares, that this landscape is so very different from that of South Carolina? That you would not, in fact, be in any way reminded of—of where you used to live?"

He stared into his empty glass for so long that she thought he was not going to answer. Then he lifted his head and looked straight at her.

"How very perceptive of you, Miss Haslam," he said, and the drawl was more noticeable than ever. "That is exactly why I stayed, and why I intend to stay."

That was all she learned that night, but it was something, she thought. A man who did not want to be reminded of the home where he had been born, who did not want even to talk of his former life, of his family or friends, but had apparently closed a door upon his past, must surely have something sinister to hide. When she found out what it was, as she was resolved to do, she would use it as a weapon, on behalf of her friends whom he had so scornfully referred to as "peasants".

That morning, Alan had risen even earlier than usual so that he could be free by mid-afternoon. Then he had groomed his pony and cleaned its tackle, washed his hair and sat patiently while Alice trimmed it for him. Dressed in his best suit, in his pocket the silver watch Jennifer had brought him back from London, he had set out to call upon the Duchy's agent at Princetown. Now he was riding back along the turnpike road, in the same pocket as the precious watch an equally precious document, the lease of Ben Cobbledick's farm. Next week he could take possession, not only of the land as it stood but also of the eight acres of newtake allowed upon a change of tenancy. He felt ten feet tall and strong enough to balance Crockern Tor upon his shoulders, *and* all the tinners who used to sit up there and make their own laws.

He was whistling as he rode but in his mind's eye he was trying to picture Jenny's face when he gave her the news. His heart felt fit to burst with love and gratitude towards her, for this change in his fortunes would not have come about if she had not so bravely gone to Hannah Sculpher's cottage on his behalf. He still had the suspicion that it was to Hannah's his mother had been going on the morning when he had followed her part way to Gibbet Tor but now he knew for certain she was not involved in Ben's death, his dreams looked like coming true, after all.

His jealousy of the American had been short-lived. The reason why Jenny had not mentioned her previous meetings with Mr Meares, Alan had decided, was because they were not important enough to her. As to that warm greeting he had witnessed so soon after she had told him she was too tired to talk, that was easily explained. The American had come to her rescue when she was in trouble and had called, as was perfectly natural, to enquire if she had recovered from her distressing experience. It would not have been like Jenny to refuse to see him, or to smile upon him in gratitude.

He was planning in his mind now what he would say to her. Unless she gave him any encouragement, he would not even hint at marriage, would not tell her that the road to success that he saw ahead of him would have no meaning if she did not travel it with him. She had been home such a short time and so much had happened, that she needed to be left in peace for a while in order to settle again to her former type of living. In fact, he decided, he would simply show her the lease. There was really no need to say anything at all.

Away to his left, the lights of Heronslea gleamed faintly at the end of the mile-long drive. He had no wish to change places with the American, living in that imposing house surrounded by its huge enclosure. For him there would be no satisfaction in the easy life, or in possessions which he had not earned by his own efforts. And he doubted if he would sleep as soundly at nights if he had behaved as ruthlessly as Darrell Meares.

Alan quickened his pony's pace as he neared the little bridge over the river, then urged it into a canter as he turned into the lane to Lidden Barton. When he reached the house he tethered the animal quickly and ran eagerly up the steps, already taking the lease from his pocket.

Mrs Westcott, who came in answer to his ring, looked completely taken aback at sight of him. "Oh, my dear days!" she exclaimed in consternation. "Here's you all dressed up for calling, and Miss Jenny not at home."

"Not at home?" He repeated the words as if they were in some foreign language which he could not understand. "But she must be. She *must* be."

"She's not, Alan, I'm telling you. Gone to Heronslea, she has."

"Heronslea?" he repeated incredulously. "She's gone to *Heronslea?*"

"That's right. She and the professor. They were invited to dinner by the American gentleman. You should have seen her, looking a fair treat she was, in a gold taffety dress she bought in London with flounces and lace, and her hair done so stylish, and carrying a painted fan. I reckon Miss Jenny'd do credit to any gentleman's dinner-table and it beats me how she came back from London unwed."

Once, as a small child, Alan had fallen into the river. He could still remember the shock of it, the icy water closing over his head, the sensation of being pressed down, carried along in the current, helpless. He had the same feeling now. He turned away, said "Thank you, Mrs Westcott" over his shoulder, and went slowly down the steps.

"Was it important, Alan, shall I tell Miss Jenny you called?"

He stood for a moment, staring down at the document in his hand. Important? To him it meant everything, this chance, small though it was, to strike out on his own. But to Jenny, who was dressed in her London finery and dining at the wealthy American's mansion?

He said tonelessly, "No thanks, Mrs Westcott. I'd rather you didn't tell her. I—I just happened to be riding this way."

"If you're sure," she said doubtfully.

"Yes, I'm quite sure," he said curtly. "Don't tell her, please."

Slowly, as if he had aged twenty years in five minutes, he untied the reins and led his pony down the path to the gate. He went through into the riverside meadow and walked for a while before mounting and setting off for home. On the hill above Wellsworthy he reined in and sat staring at the fork in the road just below him. One way led to Ben Cobbledick's farm and towards his own home. The other led to Dartmeet, and just beyond Dartmeet lived Nan Webber. He would receive a welcome there, no doubt of it. If he should show Nan Webber the lease of Stadden he knew what *her* reaction would be. Within five minutes she'd picture herself installed there.

And why not? Why not accept the girl who was ready for the taking, the girl his mother, and other people, he supposed, considered much more suited to be his wife than Jennifer Haslam? Why cling to this ridiculous, impossible dream? Jenny was not for him. She never would be. Once, perhaps, there had been a faint chance, before she went to London. Even now, if it were not for the American . . . The two factors combined made the odds against him too heavy. It was best to accept that, and put an end to hope.

He rode on towards home and stabled his pony quietly so that no one would know he had returned, then slipped the leash from his bitch's collar and calling her softly to follow, took the sheep track which wound up behind the farm. Leaning on the gate of his father's top field, the collie's warm body pressed against his leg, he faced, for the second time, the bitter endings of his dreams.

Darrell stood in front of his mahogany wardrobe, running his eye along the row of clothes. Behind him Big Jacob, who had been born on the plantation in South Carolina, waited patiently to fulfill his rôle of valet. He had played many parts since leaving home with his young master two years ago. He had been personal servant, confidant, even whipping-boy during Darrel's black moods. His understanding and patience were unlimited. There had been times when both were sorely tried, and not only by his master. There were places, he had discovered, many places, where even as a servant he was banned from entry and referred to contemptuously as a no-good nigger straight out of the jungle.

But not here, not on Dartmoor. The moormen revered physical strength and Jacob was very strong. Unknown to Darrell he had enjoyed a bout or two of wrestling with the local champions. The women regarded him with awe and not a little fear. He supposed they did not realize that they had less to fear from him than from one of these drunken miners who his master had hired to work on this new type of plantation. One of the first lessons he had been taught was that his life was forfeit if he so much as laid a finger on a white woman.

He shivered in the chill of the September morning. The sun had not yet penetrated the mist which seemed to envelope this wild, alien country every morning, getting into Jacob's bones, making him feel an old man at forty.

Darrell turned. "You feel the cold, Jacob?"

"Yes, suh. Don't you?"

Darrell shrugged. "I'll get used to it."

Jacob sighed. "You mean to stay, then, suh?"

"Of course. I've sunk a great deal of money in

this place. I can't keep on wandering for ever. Besides . . ."

Besides, he said to himself, he had a reason now for staying, a real reason. There was the girl, that little spitfire who more than once had tried to put him in his place. In his mind's eye he could picture her, the colour rushing into her cheeks, her eyes wide and very bright, chin up, hands clenched. By God, she was attractive when she was angry. *And* when she was tipsy, he recalled with a smile, for she had been very amusing then, trying hard to retain her dignity while alternating between hiccups and giggles. He'd wanted to kiss her then, and on the evening she came to dinner. That evening he'd wanted to bring her up here to his bedroom when her passion was already roused by anger. But even had her father not been there, Darrell had a suspicion he would not get young Jennifer Haslam to bed without a ring on her finger. So be it, then. Heronslea should have a mistress and one who would ensure that neither the house nor its master should ever be dull, Or lonely . . .

"I'll wear the dark suit," he said, "it's more appropriate for a Sunday."

"You are going out, suh?" asked Jacob, taking the coat and trousers from their hangers.

"I intend calling on Professor Haslam and his daughter and inviting them to share my carriage to the church at Widecombe. I dare say Miss Haslam will find some reason why she should not do so, but for her father's sake ..."

"She will accept your invitation," Jacob finished when Darrell paused. "She is a very pretty young lady, suh, and with plenty of spirit. Like your new horse," he added, smiling.

"That was not very tactful, Jacob. I took a toss from that stubborn creature. I do not intend to suffer the same humiliation at the hands of Miss Haslam."

"No, suh," Jacob said gravely. "The ladies of your family have had plenty of spirit, but the men have always been the masters."

Darrell realized that the Negro was right, although he himself had never given the matter any thought, taking it for granted. Now, pulling on his trousers, he recalled Sunday mornings at home, the carriage drawn up before the white portico, his mother resplendent in white dress and hat, carrying a white parasol—she always wore white for church-going—the chattering of his young sisters in the bedrooms above, and then his father appearing, watch in hand. He remembered the girls, running down the stairs in a flurry of pink and blue skirts and frilled petticoats, scurrying past their father, nearly falling over themselves in the scramble to be first into the carriage. Then his father's voice, sounding like thunder:

"You are one minute late. If this occurs next Sunday you will remain at home and the congregation will learn the reason. There *are* people it is admissable to keep waiting, but God is not one of them and neither am I."

Holding out his arms for Jacob to put on his coat, Darrell looked down at the wide sweep of gravel in front of the house. Would he one day wait there for *his* daughters? Could he seriously be contemplating breaking his resolve? After what had happened two years ago he had intended to cut himself off from any emotional involvement, never to marry, never to have children—unless accidentally by one of the women with whom he had amused himself from time to time. He had faced tragedy once, and only just survived. If it should strike again . . .

"You wish the carriage to be brought round now, suh?" asked Jacob, breaking into Darrell's thoughts.

"Yes, Jacob, and make sure there are some rugs in it. Professor and Miss Haslam may be used to this climate but I have no intention of arriving at church with my knees knocking from the cold."

"No, suh," said Jacob, chuckling as he handed hat and gloves to his master. "It would not make a good impression on the young lady you are intending to court."

"Who the devil said anything about courting her? There are times, Jacob, when you presume too far."

"Yes, suh," the Negro said meekly, and went quietly from the room.

Darrell laughed to himself. It was no good thinking he could hide anything from Big Jacob, and the new eagerness for life which he was feeling this morning must be only too obvious.

As his carriage lurched and swayed on its way up the rough lane to Lidden Barton, Darrell tried to imagine how he would be received by Jennifer. He was too experienced with women not to know that despite her outbursts of anger and scorn, she was very much attracted by him. He felt sure that once he had her in his arms and was kissing her as he guessed she had not been kissed while in London, she would soon forget all that nonsense about the imaginary rights of a lot of unimportant small farmers and rabbit-catchers.

When the carriage reached the driveway, Darrell was astonished to see there were a dozen or so saddle horses tethered beneath the trees, and several young men talking to Jennifer on the steps of the house. She was wearing a plain grey gown and her hair was simply dressed and partly covered by a white cap. Except for the manner in which she was talking, she could have been an exceptionally young housekeeper.

Ordering his coachman to remain on the box, Darrell got down from his carriage and approached the house. The young men, and they were as young as Jennifer herself, Darrell saw with a stab of annoyance, turned to stare with scarcely veiled curiosity, while Jennifer broke off in mid-sentence with a gasp—of dismay, he suspected.

Mounting the steps, Darrell removed his hat and bowed. "Good morning, Miss Haslam. I fear I have perhaps called at a most inopportune moment."

Swiftly she recovered her composure. "Not at all, Mr Meares," she said coolly. "Am I to understand that my father invited you? If so, I am afraid he did not tell me."

Puzzled, he said, "You have it the wrong way round. The invitation was to come from me, to take you and your father to church."

She looked completely taken aback at his words. Sensing an awkward situation, the young men discreetly withdrew into the house, to Darrell's satisfaction.

"I'm so sorry," Jennifer said, "if there has been a misunderstanding. Papa and I are not attending church. We have this—this meeting, you see."

A gathering of people at a private house and a Sunday morning. Jennifer's simple grey dress, the plain hair style and little cap. Darrell put two and two together and thought, they must be Quakers, though I should never have suspected it.

As if reading his thoughts, she said, "It is not a religious meeting, although Mr Taverner, who is a retired parson, gives a blessing and says a prayer or two. Those young men you saw are members of a reading party from Oxford University who are staying on Dartmoor. We entertain them here so that they can exchange views with the local experts such as Papa, and Mr Taverner, and Lady Cleave who is knowledgeable about the moorland plants, and—oh, here she is!"

Darrell saw a two-wheeled farmcart, drawn by a moorland pony, coming down the lane. Driving it was the young farmer who had said he had been a pupil of Professor Haslam's and had so annoyed Darrell by his impertinence. On an improvised seat of straw bales sat an elderly woman enveloped in a voluminous black cloak lined with red. A tattered black straw hat, decorated with red ribbons, was perched lopsidedly on her straggly white hair. She was waving gaily to Jennifer, who hurried down the steps to meet her.

"Jenny, my dear, how good it is to see you home again!" Lady Cleave greeted her. "And how well you look, and prettier than ever. I want to hear all about your adventures in London, but first . . . Oh, thank you, Alan," she interrupted herself as the farmer helped her down. "It *was* so kind of you to fetch me. I have to admit that at last my old legs are becoming stiff. But my brain is still as active as ever, praise be, and I am so looking forward to . . . Dear me, this is a face I don't recognize!" she exclaimed, as she saw Darrell.

Before Jennifer could introduce him, Lady Cleave started talking again. "I can guess who you are, I think. You're the naughty American who has destroyed one of the rarest plants on this part of the moor. I've been intending to call on you and express my extreme displeasure. The least you could have done before you uprooted everything within sight to plant your wretched little trees was to ensure that you were not ruining the habitat of those specimens which it has taken me years to discover and protect."

In his astonishment, Darrell forgot to bow, even to remove his hat. And then, as he saw what was occurring in the driveway, he gave no more thought to this eccentric old woman, or even to Jennifer. Young Vicary was backing his cart towards Darrell's carriage. A few more yards and . . .

"It's perfectly all right, Mr Meares," said Jennifer beside him. "Alan knows exactly what he's doing."

"The devil he does!" Darrell exclaimed, and shouting to the young man to stop at once, rushed headlong down the steps.

Startled, the pony reared, then plunged forward. A shaft caught Alan Vicary on the shoulder and knocked him to the ground. He was up in a moment and had grabbed the reins but it was too late to prevent pandemonium breaking out amongst the tethered saddle-horses. Whinnying and snorting, they tried to break free, bumping into one another, kicking and bucking, while Darrell's coachman struggled to retain control of the two carriage horses as the cart banged into the side of the vehicle.

Jennifer ran down the steps and, joined by the half-witted lad whose part she had taken, quickly untied the more troublesome of the saddle-horses and tethered them further away, while Alan quietened the frightened pony.

Lady Cleave said, "That was extremely stupid of you, Mr Meares. You might have caused a very serious accident."

He turned to glare up at her. "*I* might have caused . . ." His anger made it impossible to finish the sentence.

"Alan, are you hurt?" Jennifer was asking anxiously.

"No, nor the pony, thank God, but it was a near thing."

"Damn you *and* your pony!" Darrell exploded. "Look what you've done to my carriage."

A panel was splintered and the paintwork had been deeply scratched along the whole of one side.

Your Vicary, tight-lipped, said, "I'm sorry about that, but it was your own fault."

"If anyone else says that, when it was evident . . ."

"What *was* evident," Jennifer said, her cheeks flushed, "was your stupidity, as Lady Cleave has just said. And this is by no means the first time that I've been made aware that you should have nothing whatever to do with horses. Alan, you were splendid," she remarked over her shoulder as she went up the steps, and then, loudly, "Lady Cleave, as I am sure it will not occur to Mr. Meares that he owes anybody an apology, I make one now, on his behalf. Shall we go inside?"

Scarcely able to control his fury, Darrell wrenched open the door to his carriage, mounted the steps and shouted to his coachman, "Get me out of here at once!"

Then, to his further humiliation, young Vicary's help was needed to turn the horses in the confined space and he could not fail to notice the contrast between the quiet, controlled manner in which the farmer completed this difficult manoeuvre, and his own explosive wrath.

Thoroughly put out, he ordered his coachman to drive him home. He was not in any mood now for church-going. At Heronslea, his unexpected return caught the servants unawares, and he came upon one of the outside workers having a romp with a housemaid on the landing. The girl fled, in a flurry of black and white. The man came shamefacedly down the stairs.

"Get out of this house immediately," Darrell ordered, only just stopping himself from striking the fellow, "and if you so much as show yourself anywhere near my grounds again. I'll set the dogs on you. Jacob. *Jacob!*" When the Negro appeared, "Help this rascal on his way," Darrell shouted and then, as Jacob, taken by surprise, went to open the front door, "Not that door, you dolt!"

The butler drew himself up and looked as if he was about to protest, then changed his mind and walked with immense dignity across the hall, the frightened workman hurrying ahead of him. By the time Jacob returned, Darrell had drunk two glasses of brandy.

"I take it you have not been to church, suh," the butler said impassively.

"Of course I've not been to church. Haven't you seen my carriage has been damaged?"

"Yes, suh. How did it happen?"

"A young idiot with one of these unmanageable wild ponies crashed into it with his farmcart."

"That was unfortunate. Even so, there is not sufficient damage to have prevented you from . . ."

"What are you getting at?" Darrell demanded.

"I think that the accident to the carriage is not the reason why you turned back. The young lady, perhaps, was not prepared—not able—to accompany you and in your disappointment . . ."

"Damn you, Jacob, you go too far!"

Darrell flung the brandy glass across the room. As it splintered against the wall beside the fireplace, a stain spread over the new wallpaper.

"Oh, my God!" he exclaimed, seeing what he had done, then slumped into a chair and put his head in his hands.

Jacob went to the wine cabinet, poured another glass of brandy and set it on a small table beside Darrell. Then he knelt, grunting a little because of the stiffness the damp moorland air had caused in his bones, and said gently, "You tell Jacob, Massa Darrell, you tell Big Jacob what really happened."

Through his spread fingers, his voice unsteady, Darrell said, "I lost my temper."

"Seems to me," the Negro said, in the same gentle tones, "that has happened many times these last two years."

"Do you wonder at it?" his master demanded, raising his head. "Haven't I every reason to . . . ?"

"For a while, yes," Jacob said in a firmer tone. "For a year, perhaps, everyone would make excuses for you. But now . . . May I speak freely?"

Darrell reached for the glass. "You damned well will, whether I say so or not. What is it?"

The Negro got up stiffly. He took a deep breath and for all his size and imposing appearance, he looked a little nervous.

"It seems to me that you are behaving as you did when you were a little boy. Always you have wanted everything your own way, all things and all people to bend to your will, and when that does not happen . . ."

He broke off, seeing his master's mouth tighten, the hand clenched menacingly.

The moment passed. Darrell said, "Yes, you're right. I behaved abominably, like the spoiled child I used to be."

"You want to tell me about it?"

Darrell shrugged. "I might as well."

When he had done so, Jacob looked thoughtful. "This young farmer—you have met him before?"

"Once only, and then briefly." He told Jacob how

he and Alan Vicary had arrived at Lidden Barton simultaneously on the day Jennifer had found the old woman hanging in the wood, and how Professor Haslam had inveigled him into the study while Vicary had gone into the parlour with Jennifer.

At that, the butler looked wise. "Ah, I understand now."

Darrell rose to his feet. "You understand what?"

"The reason for your black mood, why you did not feel like going to church."

"Do you, indeed?" said Darrell sarcastically. "Are you prepared to share this knowledge with me?"

"Certainly, suh, if you wish. It is simple, an old story, as old as the world itself. One young woman, two young men who desire her . . ."

"*What*?" Darrell's voice rose. "Are you daring to suggest that I am jealous of a clod-footed hobbledy-hoy?"

Jacob put his head on one side. "If he was just that, suh, I don't think Miss Haslam would even contemplate . . ."

"Oh, you'd be surprised what she contemplates, Jacob, *and* by the people she chooses for friends. A daughter of that—that rabbit-catcher up on the hill, a common labourer who builds walls,—an eccentric old woman who blathered on about some useless plant I'm supposed to have dug up." He began to pace the room. "I've a damned good mind to pack up and move on."

The Negro sighed heavily. "And what would that

solve? We have been moving on for two whole
years now. First Italy, then France, Spain, Germany,
now England, and it has brought you no nearer . . ."

"Nearer what?" Darrell questioned sharply as
Jacob hesitated.

"Learning to live with what happened. Running
away won't alter anything, Massa Darrell, it won't
bring them back."

Darrell paused in his pacing and looked out of
the window. The sun was already too far round to
give any warmth to this room. That had been one
of his biggest mistakes, to face the house as if he
was still in a hot country.

"Then what do you suggest?" he asked, a note of
hopelessness in his voice.

Jacob did not answer at once. He knew what he
was about to say would not be well received but it
had to be said, he believed.

"I think you should tell Miss Haslam about what
happened two years ago."

Darrell swung round, hands clenched at his sides.
"The devil you do! For what purpose, to make her
sorry for me?"

"That was not the intention, suh."

"What, then?"

"There is a saying, I believe, that to understand
is to forgive. If Miss Haslam understood . . ."

"I don't want forgiveness, damn you! If there's
any forgiving to be done, it's I who will do it and
she who'll do the seeking."

"Yes, suh, but for what?" Jacob asked quietly.

"For—for setting herself against me, from the very beginning, for being so deuced impertinent and —and . . ."

As Darrell strode from the room, Jacob shook his head sadly and finished the sentence, softly to himself, "and daring even to look at any other man."

Chapter Five

"I can't imagine why I didn't think of this solution before," Jennifer told Mollie. "Lady Cleave has spoken to me several times about her barrister cousin who has earned a reputation for championing the cause of the weak and helpless against those who seek to oppress them. And now he's moved to Plymouth . . .".

"You've actually asked Lady Cleave to bring the Heronslea enclosure to his notice?"

"I didn't even have to ask her. As soon as I told her what had been happening, she suggested it. Mr Meares had already aroused her hostility by destroying some rare plant she's been cherishing for years, and by his appalling behaviour in our driveway."

"So what do you think will happen next?"

"It depends on Sir Robert Bratton. Apparently a few years ago he began to delve into the legality of the way in which the Duchy were granting leases for big amounts of land to be enclosed, and then he had to drop it because of being involved fully in more urgent enquiries."

"Suppose he finds Mr Meares' lease is perfectly legal?"

"It can't be, Mollie, if it infringes age-old rights and privileges. This is what I keep trying to tell Darrell Meares but it's hopeless. He says he won't believe any such rights exist unless he is presented with legal documents proving them. How can your father or any of the others do that without help and advice? And can you imagine poor Zebedee waving a piece of paper with a seal attached to prove he has a right to pick a handful of whortleberries?"

Mollie laughed at that, then asked seriously, "So you are still set on opposing the American?"

"Of course," Jennifer answered, surprised by the question. "Have you ever known me to go back on anything I've set my mind to?"

"It's different now, though, isn't it? I mean, you've become involved with him personally."

"Just because he happened to come to my aid after I'd had that awful shock?"

"But you've been to Heronslea to dinner, haven't you?"

"That doesn't make any difference. I made my attitude perfectly clear to him."

"Does this mean you don't feel attracted to him any more?"

Jennifer was rocking the cradle with her foot. The movement ceased as she answered, "I—didn't say that." She looked across at her friend, a worried expression on her face. "Mollie, do you think it's possible to be a little in love with someone you don't even like?"

"It may be possible for you, Jenny, it certainly wouldn't be for me. But then, as I've said before, life's much more complicated for you. It's bound to be, when you think of your parents, how entirely different from each other they were in temperament and upbringing."

"Yet there was no doubt it was a happy marriage."

"Don't you know why? It was because your mother asked so little and gave so much. Although your father can be a pet, and I've every reason to be grateful to him for giving me free lessons when I was a child, he *is* self-centered, and only someone like your mother . . ."

"But I'm not like her, am I?"

"In many ways you are. You like to give, Jenny, but you are very fond of your own way and sometimes you can be as ruthless as your father."

"Ruthless? That's a strong word."

"Too strong to apply to your quarrel with Mr Meares?"

"*My* quarrel? I don't call that a fair accusation. You know very well I've set myself up against him on behalf of the commoners—*and* on your father's behalf, you might remember."

"Yes, originally."

"What do you mean by that?"

Mollie shrugged. "I think it's become more personal now. I think the fact that you *do* find him attractive has made you angry out of all proportion and that's what I meant by ruthless."

"Well, I like that! It was you who said you wished he'd broken his neck when his horse threw him, I'd like to remind you. She rocked the cradle so vigorously that the baby woke and started to cry. "Oh, dear, I'm sorry. Can I pick him up?"

"Yes, if you want. In fact," said Mollie somewhat forcefully, "I think it might be a good idea—for you, I mean."

"What's behind that remark?" Jennifer asked as she lifted her godson on to her lap.

"Never you mind," Mollie said maddeningly, as she rose to make up the fire. Her back to Jennifer, she asked in a carefully casual tone, "Does Mr Meares like children?"

"I haven't the faintest idea. How should I know that?"

"I just wondered."

"You can go on wondering, then. I *don't* know, and I really am not interested. Now, can we change the subject? I came, if you recall, to discuss the christening."

"So you did," said Mollie placidly. "I wonder how we strayed from that to talking about the American. It seems to happen each time you come."

"Any more of that kind of talk and you can find

another godmother for William," Jennifer declared. Then, seeing Mollie's expression, she said, contritely, "You know very well I didn't mean that. I *am* being touchy, aren't I? But I feel all at sea, Mollie. I thought I was coming home to find things exactly as they were, and instead . . ."

"I know, love," said Mollie, putting an arm around Jennifer's shoulders and kissing her cheek. "You've had a series of shocks since your return. I was only teasing, I didn't mean to upset you. William's almost asleep again. Shall I put him back in the cradle or do you want to go on nursing him?"

"I—I'd like to keep him a bit longer, if you don't mind."

"All right. I'll go and give Tom a call to come in for tea."

The baby's body was warm against Jennifer, its head a light weight on her breast. She thought, perhaps Mollie was testing me. Perhaps this *is* the real test, trying to imagine having a baby by a man you think yourself in love with. But instead of Darrell Meares, into her mind came a picture of Alan, whose strong, work-roughened hands could be so gentle with all young and helpless creatures, babies or lambs, or birds which had fallen from nests.

Yet that couldn't be the whole answer, surely? There was more to marriage than having babies. She knew now that Mollie couldn't help her. No one could. It was something she would have to find out for herself.

Mrs Vicary was making pastry, while Bertha peeled apples at the other end of the table, bleached with years of scrubbing. They greeted Jennifer while continuing with their tasks.

"You'll not find Alan here today," his mother said. "He and his father set out early to take the cattle down to the in-country. Sit you down, though, and I'll mash some tea so soon as I've got this pie ready for baking."

"Can't I help?" Jennifer asked.

"Not in those fine clothes," Mrs Vicary said, eyeing Jennifer's blue riding-habit. "But if you'm so anxious, you can get out the cups and saucers. They'm in . . ."

"The dresser cupboard," Jennifer said. "You see, I haven't forgotten. Were they your own cattle or the ones on summer pasture?"

"Our own. A nice bunch, Alan reckons, and should fetch a good price. That'll see us through the winter, likely, unless it turn out a hard one."

Jennifer set out cups and saucers and tried to draw Bertha into conversation but the girl, as always when her mother was present, was subdued.

"I hear you had a big "do" at your place on Sunday," Mrs Vicary remarked. "Alan said you scarce had a moment to speak to him."

"I hardly had time to speak to anybody. Ada's still not back with us and Mrs Westcott and I were almost buried under mountains of food and washing-up."

"London's not made you shy of work then?"

"Good gracious, no! I was glad to get back to doing something really useful. I spent so much time in London just filling in the hours, it was boring." She moved the big black kettle on to the hottest part of the range and reached up to the mantelshelf for the tea caddy. "Is the milk in the dairy?"

"That's right. And bring in a bowl of cream to have with the scones."

Over tea, Bertha found her voice. "Alan told us there was a fine old rumpus in your driveway and that the American gentleman's carriage got damaged, and he went off in a rage."

"That's true," Jennifer agreed, "but then, Mr Meares is often in a rage."

Mrs Vicary glanced up. "I thought you were friends with him, you and your father."

Jennifer shrugged. "Papa finds him interesting to talk to."

"Don't you? I should have thought he's the kind of gentleman you'd met in London."

"I never met anyone like Mr Meares in London," Jennifer said firmly. "These scones are delicious, Mrs Vicary. I shall soon be putting on so much weight I shan't be able to get into the clothes I bought up there."

"You'm much slimmer than Nan Webber, though," Bertha declared. "She was nearly bursting out of her blouse when Alan took her down to look at Ben Cobbledick's place."

"When was that?" her mother asked sharply.

"Yesterday evening," Bertha, encouraged for once, rushed on. "I was that surprised because I thought Alan reckoned that wicked rumour about him killing old Ben had been started by Nan or by her father. Course, we've been seeing quite a bit of Nan while you've been away, Jenny. Mam thought . . ."

"Never you mind what I thought," Mrs Vicary said sternly. "I expect Alan's so proud of having got the place that he wants everyone . . ."

"Having got the place?" Jennifer repeated in surprise. "You mean, it's been settled?"

It was Mrs Vicary's turn to look surprised. "Why, yes, nearly a week since. Didn't he tell you?"

Jennifer lowered her head, not wanting to betray the hurt she felt. "No, he didn't, but then, as you said, I hardly had time to speak to him on Sunday. I expect he thought I was too busy to take in such splendid news."

She could have accepted it, believing he had been waiting to choose just the right moment, if she had not just learned that Nan Webber had been told before her. Had Alan lied to her about Nan? Or was he playing some kind of double game? No, not Alan, surely, he had always been so open and honest.

She made an effort and asked brightly, "Has he decided when he'll take over?"

"In a few days. He'll be living at home still, of course. There's a lot to do down there. Old Ben had let the place go. 'Tisn't right for any man to do for himself, he needs a woman to . . ."

"Nan'd step in and look after Alan tomorrow if he'd say the word," Bertha said.

Mrs Vicary looked about to reprimand her daughter. Then, changing her mind, she said, "He could do worse. Been raised to farm work, has Nan, and taught to take care of the pennies. She'm a good-tempered little maid, too."

"Alan'd have to watch her with other boys, though," Bertha ventured, and giggled.

"You mind your tongue, maid," her mother warned. "That's no way to be talking, especially in front of Jenny. You'm making hard work of that scone after all," she added, turning to Jennifer.

Jennifer looked down at her plate and saw that, without knowing she was doing so, she had crumbled the scone into tiny pieces. She was feeling as she had done on her first day home, when she had been given dinner in the Vicary's parlour. She had been made welcome then, as she was now, but there was an undercurrent which she had not known in the old days. True, she had never felt completely at ease with Alan's mother and Mrs Vicary was not a woman to encourage a close relationship. Then how would I like her for a mother-in-law, Jennifer thought, facing the idea for the first time. If all this talk about Nan is mere speculation, *if* I were to marry Alan, the Vicarys would be my family as well as his, and this farm, after Papa's death, my second home.

She finished the scone, then rose and said, "I'd better be getting back. Papa wants me to do some copying out for him this evening."

"Do you want me to give Alan a message?" Mrs Vicary asked, at the door.

"No, thank you. Except—perhaps you'd tell him how glad I am, about his having Ben's place, and when he can spare the time . . ."

"He'll not have much spare time ahead of him. They'm behind with the sheep dipping and then they've to take the agistered cattle off the moor and down to their owners in the in-country. And then, there'll be all the work he'll be wanting to get on with at Stadden."

"Yes. Yes, of course. Thank you for giving me tea, Mrs Vicary."

Jennifer intended to ride straight home and immerse herself in the work her father wanted done. But when she came to the track which led to Ben's farm, she found herself, without conscious thought, turning the mare's head in that direction. A neighbour had taken Ben's dog, and the few cattle had been sold to pay for the old man's burial. His ponies were still grazing up on the open moor but at the October drift they would probably be rounded up and sent to the annual sale at Chagford. Who would benefit from their sale, or that of Ben's few belongings, nobody seemed to know. It was sad to think of people like him and Hannah Sculpher, living alone for so long without any relatives in the world that anyone knew about.

Thinking along those lines reminded Jennifer that she had not yet visited her grandfather who lived near the stone quarries some miles beyond Cock Tor. Not that he lived alone, for he had Aunt Sarah, his spinster daughter, to look after him. Jennifer had thought she would have all the time in the world when she returned from London but she had not anticipated being faced with so much work for her father or Ada being away, or so many unexpected things happening. And one of the most unexpected, and niggling still at her mind, was Alan's delay in telling her he was to take over Ben's holding, especially as had it not been for her intervention, his suspicions about his mother would have stopped him even applying for the lease. She thought back to Sunday. Certainly she had been busy, but not so occupied that he could not have found an opportunity had he wanted. Then why hadn't he done so?

When she reached the farm, she regretted the impulse which had brought her for it was depressing in its deserted state, with no sound but the ripple of the stream and the chirruping of sparrows from the dilapidated cattle shed. Then, taking her completely by surprise, she heard a woman singing. Tuneless but cheerful, it came from inside the house.

As Jennifer approached. Nan Webber appeared at the back door, a pail in her hand. She was making for the privy but, at sight of Jennifer, stopped short.

"Why, 'tis Miss Haslam!" she exclaimed, pushing the hair out of her eyes. "Whatever be you doing here?"

"I—I just came to have a look."

"Oh, I see—just to have a look." The girl's gaze went slowly over the mare which Zebedee kept so well groomed, over Jennifer's smart riding-habit and little hat with its feather trimming, then back to the pail of dirty water she was carrying. Then she smiled and to Jennifer it seemed a strange smile in the circumstances, almost of triumph.

"Well," she said amiably, "I'm sure you'm welcome, but 'tis proper mucky. I'm trying to clean it up a bit, to give Alan a surprise like. A bit down in the dumps he was, last evening, seeing what state the house was in but I told un 'twouldn't take long to set it to rights, given plenty of soap and water, and a pair of willing hands."

The words were spoken in the friendliest of tones. Nan's freckled face, framed by golden curls, was as guileless as a child's. Yet Jennifer felt as if she were having knives stuck into her. Behind the seemingly innocent façade she was aware of envy and malice.

Her smile as false as Nan's, she said, "I won't hinder you, then. I'm sure Alan will be delighted when he sees what you've done."

"That's why I be doing it," Nan said simply. "Good-day to you, then, Miss Haslam."

She was talking, Jennifer thought, as if she were

already mistress here, politely getting rid of an un-
welcome visitor. She could almost feel Nan's satisfaction as she turned Bracken's head and set off
back along the track.

When she neared Mollie's house she was tempted
to stop and have a talk with her friend. Perhaps if
she tried to put her muddled thoughts into words, it
would help to clear her mind. But Tom would be
finishing work soon, and it was near the baby's
feeding time. She suddenly felt shut out, from Alan's
home and from the farm he was about to take over,
even from Mollie's cottage.

Annoyed by this unfamiliar attack of self-pity,
she urged Bracken into a fast canter and soon they
had breasted the hill and were within sight of
Heronslea. Her thoughts turned then to Darrell
Meares but her feelings towards him were muddled,
too. She was thankful when she reached home and
found that the work her father had prepared for her
was so complicated that it occupied the whole of
her mind until dinner time. Afterwards, her father
asked her to read to him, admitting that his sight
was beginning to fail and he found reading by lamplight too much of a strain.

"For the first time, I was rather dreading the
winter," he confessed. "Having you home again will
make all the difference."

She gave him a hug, immensely grateful for his
words of appreciation, coming at a time when she
most needed them. They reassured her that here,

at least, in the relationship with her father, nothing had changed and she was still needed. Tomorrow she would visit her grandfather and Aunt Sarah and that would be equally reassuring. Their lives were as peaceful as the moor on a calm summer's day and as unchanging as the granite tors.

Instead of riding to visit her grandfather, Jennifer sat beside the parlour fire, glad not only of its warmth but also of the cheerful flicker of flames on such a dark and dismal morning. Some time in the night it had started to rain and by the time she woke, the river had risen about a foot and now was rushing between the boulders, the water churned into foam in the eddies beneath the fern-grown banks.

She was free of housework today because Ada had returned soon after breakfast, reporting that her mother had made a good recovery, and as Jennifer's father did not need her help at present, it seemed a good opportunity to write to Aunt Lucy.

Life here is not without its excitements, she wrote, then paused, trying to visualize her aunt's face as she read that her niece had come upon a reputed black witch who had hanged herself, or about a local feud with a rich American.

Jennifer knew whose side Aunt Lucy would take in that affair, and if her aunt learned that the American was also a bachelor, she would be all for Jennifer setting her cap at him as her only chance of making a suitable marriage "in that dreadful backward part of the country in which your misguided father saw fit to bring you up."

So, instead, she wrote, *There are plans afoot for the Queen to visit the fleet at Plymouth and it is said the Prince Consort may inspect the naptha works at the old prison at Princetown.*

Because her spirits this morning reflected the weather and life seemed suddenly full of unresolved doubts and problems, Jennifer wished for once that she could be more like Aunt Lucy, skimming along on the surface of life, with nothing more important to worry about than whether her lap dog was off its food or whether cook had put enough salt in the soup.

Her letter finished, Jennifer put away her writing materials and went across to the window to see if there seemed any chance of the weather improving. Darrell Meares, his coat soaked, water dripping from the brim of his beaver hat, was tethering his horse to the gate-post. Jennifer rang for Ada, telling her to open the door at once, for surely only a matter of great urgency could have brought him out on such a morning. Then her heart sank as she realized the reason for his visit might well be that he had heard from Lady Cleave's cousin, and had suspected she might be behind this latest move in the campaign against him.

To her relief his voice sounded calm and pleasant as Ada let him into the hall. He apologized for being so wet and thanked the maid for offering to take his coat and dry it off by the kitchen range. Then, in answer to Ada's question, he said, "It is Miss Haslam I would like to see. Will you present my compliments and say . . ."

"There is no need," Jennifer said from the parlour doorway. "You had better come to the fire, Mr Meares."

"Thank you." He gave her a formal bow. "I apologize for my appearance, and the mud . . ."

"We are used to mud on Dartmoor," she said, and was annoyed with herself for thinking that, even with his cravat looking limp and slightly askew, his face wet with rain and a splash of mud on one cheek, he was still incredibly handsome. "Would you care for some refreshment?"

"Thank you, no—at least, not yet, not until . . ." Avoiding her eyes, he spoke more quickly than usual. "The fact is, Miss Haslam, I realize that I ought to have come before now but I had business in Exeter. Doubtless you have been expecting me . . ."

"Why should you think that?" she asked warily.

"Because obviously I owe you an apology."

"For what?"

"My behaviour on Sunday. I lost my temper and . . ."

"It does seem to be rather a habit of yours," she said coolly, relieved to learn the reason for his call, "and the apology, I suggest, is due to Mr Vicary rather than to me."

"Yes, well, I—I do not know where to find Mr Vicary."

"I can easily direct you there, or you may prefer to write. Mr Vicary is able to read, you know, although you probably regard him as a peasant."

He looked up, seemed about to make a sharp retort, then said instead, "I suppose I deserved that. You are not making this very easy."

"Did you expect me to do so?"

"I had hoped for some—some degree of understanding."

"*Understanding?* How am I supposed to understand the behaviour of a so-called gentleman who insults my friends, deliberately provokes me into saying things I afterwards regret, and acts like a spoiled child when his plans are upset?"

"Yes, you are right," he agreed surprisingly. "That is exactly what Jacob said."

"Jacob?"

"My butler."

The Negro, she thought with astonishment. He allows his coloured servant to talk to him like that? This man was full of surprises, and as for understanding him . . .

"Miss Haslam, I would like to mention in my own defence, that my bad temper—for which I am fully prepared to admit there is no real excuse—was caused by disappointment. I had so looked forward to having the pleasure of your company on the drive to church. Since coming to England, in fact, since leaving Carolina, I have not met—that is to say, no young lady has held such attraction for me as you, and so . . .”

Jennifer's resentment vanished like snow beneath the sun. Part of her mind sounded a warning, telling her that this man knew exactly how to win over a woman and that his change of tactics was calculated and for some purpose of his own, but it did not matter. False though they might prove, she was gratified by his words. And so she accepted them, or at least made a pretence of doing so, changing to her “London” manner as easily as she changed her clothes.

“I am flattered, Mr Meares, and it would be churlish of me not to suggest, after such an explanation, that we forget the incident.”

“Except, naturally, my apology to Mr Vicary. Thank you, that is most generous. And now, since you were kind enough to offer . . .”

“Some wine? Of course.” She rang for Ada, and sitting down by the fire, motioned him to the chair opposite.

He remained standing, and she saw that he was staring at the portrait of her mother which hung beside the fireplace.

“I noticed these paintings the other evening but your father held my attention and so I could not take a close look at them. May I do so now?”

"Certainly. They are the work of a young man who . . ."

"Oh, I know whose work they are. At least, I should be very surprised if I were mistaken. May I take them down?"

He was still examining them when Ada brought in wine and biscuits. Then, replacing them on their hooks, he said, "Yes, I am right. They are some of Simon Casper's earliest works, I should imagine. Would it be impertinent to ask how you came by them?"

"They were . . ." She broke off, suddenly realizing the implication of what he had said. "Do you mean that you have seen other paintings by him, that he has become . . ."

"Famous? Indeed, yes. Did you not know?"

She shook her head. "While I was in London, I made enquiries but . . ."

"I dare say he is not well known in London. His studio is in Paris and most of his exhibitions held there. But if you did not buy them in London . . . Surely, not locally?"

"I did not buy them at all, Mr Meares. They were painted here. Do you not recognize the little footbridge over the river?"

He looked again at the one of herself, standing on the bridge.

"Why, yes, now that you point it out. Does this mean that he actually came here, to paint . . . ?"

"The peasants?" she said lightly. "Yes, that's

right. The child in that one is myself. The other portrait is of my mother. The young man was staying in Princetown and had lost his way. Mama was far more concerned at how thin he was and that he should sample her clotted cream and strawberry jam than about sitting for him. In fact, I don't think either of us was very interested at being painted. I didn't like standing still, and Mama wanted to get on with her gardening. But she was such a kind person . . ."

"And with a sense of humour, I should imagine," Darrell said, sipping his wine as he looked again at the portrait.

"Oh, yes. She would have been amused to think she had been painted by someone who has become famous—that she might even have been hung in an exhibition."

He said seriously, "If you did not know that, then presumably you had not realized what these paintings are worth now."

"In money, do you mean?"

He nodded, then sat down, looking thoughtful. "I would hazard a guess that separately they would fetch—oh, around a hundred guineas each. The pair somewhat more, two hundred and fifty, say. Not, of course," he added hastily, "that you would ever think of selling them."

"Naturally not. At least, certainly not the one of Mama. I am not so fond of the other. It seems artificial to me, not like the river and the moorland beyond, as I see it."

"It is an artist's romantic impression, Miss Haslam. Should you, by any chance, ever wish to sell that one—though I think it would be a pity—you would have no difficulty in finding a buyer."

A hundred guineas, she thought. What would I do with a hundred guineas, or Papa, for that matter? Neither of us really wants for anything, at least not anything that would make us any happier or more comfortable than we are. It was people like Alan who needed ready money. To stock his farm, to pay Ned Hext for building the walls of the new-take, to buy winter fodder for his beasts, to enlarge and improve the farm building and house, and for all the furniture and utensils that would be needed. For Nan Webber to use? The idea was like a stab of pain.

She asked quickly, to divert her mind, "Are you knowledgeable about paintings, Mr Meares?"

He shrugged. "I have acquired a smattering of knowledge about many subjects these last two years. Archaeology, for instance, which has given me the benefit of your father's acquaintance."

"He seems to think you know a great deal."

"I have become adept at the game of bluff, or to put it another way, adopting a façade."

"But why?" she asked, refilling his glass. "Why should you need to do that?"

"For—self-protection." He was staring at the toe

of his boot, as if he found it of absorbing interest.

Jennifer recalled that she believed he had something to hide and that if she could discover what it was, she might be provided with a weapon against him. She remained silent, afraid to probe but hoping he would go on talking.

"You asked me, during the evening you came to dinner," he said reflectively, "whether my real reason for choosing to live on Dartmoor was because it is so entirely different from my former home in South Carolina and therefore I would not be constantly reminded of—of . . ."

"Yes," she murmured encouragingly as he paused. "I remember, and you told me I was right."

He went on staring at his boot while sipping his wine. At last he said, "And so you were. It is a form of self-protection."

"Because your memories are—painful?" she ventured.

He nodded. The closed look came back into his face and she thought that was all he intended to disclose. Then suddenly he looked across at her and smiled, although it was a bleak kind of smile which did not touch his eyes.

"Big Jacob, who has known me all my life and enjoys the privileges of long service to my family, tells me it is not wise to lock past unhappiness away and refuse to face it or talk about it."

"I think Jacob is right, but we do not all think alike. You have known great unhappiness, then?"

"Such as few men have been called upon to bear." Putting down his glass, he rose abruptly and walked across to the window. With his back to her he said, in a rush of words quite unlike his usual slow drawl, "My mother and father and my two young sisters were drowned, all at the same time, in the river which flows past our plantation."

Jennifer sat absolutely still, too numbed with shock to move or even speak. The dismay she felt was made worse by the fact that this revelation was so totally unlike anything she had imagined, and by the recollection that she had thought to use his secret as a weapon against him.

At last the silence, broken only by the crackle of the fire and the patter of rain against the window, became unbearable, and she asked, "How—how did it happen?"

"They had been on an outing to Charleston, along with other families from further up the river. I had stayed behind because two of the overseers were down with fever and the third was a new man, unused to the work. When they were due back, I went down to the jetty. The paddle-steamer came around the bend in the river. I could see my father, ordering everybody about as usual, my mother's blue silk parasol, my two sisters standing by the rail, waving. Then, for no apparent reason, the boat swung around in mid-stream, listed heavily and began to capsize. I remember . . ." He paused, and she saw his hands clench at his sides. "I remember the water closing over my head as I dived into the river. Then—then someone clasping my hands, thanking me for rescuing two children. And, after that, nothing, nothing at all until I reached the house and Jacob was closing the shutters. Closing the shutters," he repeated, "but not against the sun. And Big Jacob was crying. It was the first time in my life I had ever seen a grown man cry. So then I knew."

Still Jennifer sat without moving, while she saw his hands slowly unclench, the set of his shoulders become less rigid. She heard him clear his throat and blow his nose. Then she rose and went to him.

"I—I don't know what to say," she whispered. "I thought, when Mama died, that my heart would break, but this . . ."

"So what did you do?" he demanded harshly, and as he faced her, his expression was angry, not sad. "What did you do, for solace?"

"I—it's difficult to remember, in proper sequence. At first I prayed, I think, and then I tried to comfort Papa, and then . . ." She took a deep breath and said steadily, "Then I went to a—a special place on the moor, a small combe where I always used to go whenever I was sad or worried. It's like a dozen other places within a few miles of here and yet . . ."

"It is your place of comfort, your landscape of the heart, to use your father's expression?"

"It *was* that," she said, and there was sadness in her voice but no rancour.

"But not now?"

"No, not now. You see, a wall has been built around it and the stream damned to draw off water to supply a new leat."

She saw the sudden glint in his eyes, the dawning comprehension. As if the words were being dragged from him, he said, "You mean—*I* have done this?"

She nodded without answering. Then, seeing the dismay which spread across his face, she said softly, "It doesn't matter any more. I've learned that consolation isn't to be found in any one place or in any one person or—or even trying to fill one's life with constant activity and interests."

"In what way can it be found, then?"

"In remembering, mostly. Just now, we talked about the day the young artist came here and as we talked, I could hear my mother's laughter and the warmth of her voice as she encouraged him to help himself to cream and strawberry jam. I lived that day all over again, recalling the happiness of it. It really isn't kind to the dead to shut them out, just as if they had never existed. Perhaps you can't accept that. Perhaps for you there is to be some different way. In any case, I had but the one loss, great though it was, to bear. I can't really imagine what it was like, to . . ."

"No," he said shortly. "No, I don't think you can. But thank you for trying. In the two years since it happened, I have never spoken of it to anyone except Jacob."

"But why not? That is just my point. Why be so determined to hide this tragedy as if it were something—shameful? Can't you see that people wonder, and speculate about your past life? Why, even I . . ."

"Even you—what?" he asked as she broke off.

"It doesn't matter. Except, that if you had told me this before . . ."

"Before what?"

She turned away, went back to the fire and poured herself another glass of wine. "I—I'd rather not say. Only—you seemed so hard, so—so arrogant and sure that everything you do is right, never prepared to listen . . ."

"And what I have just told you alters your opinion?"

"It—it has helped me to understand. Isn't that what you intended? But I do so wish you had told me earlier."

For by now Lady Cleave would surely have been in touch with her cousin and once he had taken up the cause of the commoners there was little likelihood that he could be dissuaded from pursuing it.

"I'm sure it's all very sad," Mollie said, "but it doesn't alter the situation, does it?"

"What do you mean?" Jennifer asked.

"Regarding what Mr Meares has done at Heronslea. Look, Jenny, Tom's parents died tragically. They were both burned to death when their cottage caught fire but . . ."

"Tom has you and the baby," Jennifer pointed out.

"He wouldn't have, if he'd behaved like Mr Meares. Tragedy should make people more understanding and sympathetic, not less so."

"Mr Meares is lonely, Mollie, that's obvious."

"Then why did he leave Carolina? He must have had some relatives there, or friends, at least."

"Not necessarily. He might have lived—well, within the family. When they died, he would have found himself alone like—like old Ben Cobbledick or Hannah Sculpher."

"Oh, Jenny! You know perfectly well there's no comparison. *They* were old and poor and they'd got into the habit of living like recluses. This American is rich, he's had every opportunity . . ."

"You can't buy yourself out of loneliness," Jennifer persisted stubbornly.

Mollie sighed. "I can see I might as well bang my head against a brick wall. So what are you going to do? Get in touch with Lady Cleave and tell her to stop her cousin investigating the legality of Mr Meares' lease?"

"I don't know," Jennifer said miserably. "I honestly don't know what to do."

"Then I'll tell you something that may help you to make up your mind." Mollie's voice was unusually harsh. "Yesterday Sam Barrett called in here. He'd been up to collect father's rabbit catch. It was only about half the usual amount and I can tell you why. Mr Meares has not only taken away part of the warren for his enclosure but he's also been putting down poison to stop the rabbits eating his seedlings."

"Oh, no!" Jennifer exclaimed in dismay.

"You know what that means, don't you?" Mollie went on. "Father's lost a sizeable part of his income and a source of good food has been destroyed. 'Tis no good Mr Meares trying to sound high-minded about saving the unemployed miners from starvation if he deliberately destroys food that could have benefited *them* as much as anybody else."

"I suppose he didn't realize . . ."

"And there's another thing," Mollie continued relentlessly. "Tom's cousin has been employed up at Heronslea as a carpenter and he's taken a fancy to one of the maidservants. Last Sunday, while Mr Meares was out—calling on you, I suppose, George slipped into the house for a kiss and a cuddle with her. There was no harm in it, I can vouch for that, knowing George. The American came home unexpectedly and caught them on the landing. He dismissed George at once, without giving him even a chance to speak for himself, and, what's more, he threatened him that if he showed his face anywhere near Heronslea again he'd set the dogs on him. *And* he ordered that—that black man to drive George out of the house."

"I—I can't believe it."

"You think George would make up such a story? And that father and Sam Barrett were lying, too? You'd rather take the side of this—this 'foreigner' than believe people you've known all your life? Jenny, why don't you face the truth? If Mr Meares was old and ugly and not young and attractive, would you be taking his side?"

"I'm not taking his side," Jennifer protested. "I'm just trying to be fair, to—to make allowances."

"Since when have you made allowances for injustice? Either a thing is right or it's wrong, Jenny. What a man has suffered in the past has nothing to do with it. I'm sorry to sound hard, but you've got to choose. If you've fallen in love with this man, which seems to be the case, and you want to throw in your lot with him, then that's your affair. But you can't have a foot in both camps. It has to be one or the other."

"But it needn't be like that!" Jennifer pressed her hands tightly together as if by that action she could make Mollie understand. "Don't you see? It's not that simple, not just plain black and white. You said yourself, when I came here on my first morning home, that I don't belong in one 'camp' or the other. I—I just . . . I can't make you see, can I?"

"No. I'm afraid you can't." Mollie's usually placid face was set in grim lines. "There's one thing *you* ought to see, very clearly. If you *do* love this American, and it goes as far as marriage, then you'll cut yourself off from all the friends—the real friends you have amongst the moor folk—and you'll break Alan's heart."

"That's not true!" Jennifer retorted angrily. 'Alan doesn't want me any more. He's got Nan Webber. She herself, *and* Alan's mother and sister, made that very plain."

Mollie gasped and started to protest but Jennifer did not stay to listen. With a swish of her blue skirt she hurried from the room and swung quickly into the saddle, shutting her ears to the voice of her friend, urgently calling her back.

Chapter Six

"Who's been trying to earn themselves a halo?" asked Alan, coming into the kitchen at Edgecombe Farm.

Mrs Vicary looked up from stirring a pan on the range. "What do you mean?"

"All that cleaning that's been done down at Ben's place."

The women looked at one another, their eyebrows raised. "Nobody from here's done any cleaning," his mother said. " 'Tis your place now and I'm not going to be accused of interfering and nor are the girls."

He rubbed his chin. "Someone's been down there. The question is, who?"

His mother went on stirring. "That shouldn't take much working out. As far as I know, there's only *one* person you've taken down there as yet."

"I've not taken anyone down."

"That's not true, Alan," Bertha put in. "I saw you, with Nan Webber."

"You certainly did not," he denied hotly. "Not down at Stadden."

"You were walking that way with her the other evening. Leastways, that's how it looked to me."

"Then you should stop jumping to conclusions. I met Nan by chance up on the hill when I was getting in the cattle. She told me there was a sheep on its back so I went over to get it on its feet again. And then, just to be companionable, I walked with her to the end of the track."

"Did you tell her you'd taken Stadden?" asked Alice, who was setting the table.

"Yes, I did mention it. After all, everybody'll know by now, I should think."

"Except Jenny," said his mother.

"She came here," Bertha put in eagerly. "She seemed proper put out, about not knowing, I mean."

Mrs Vicary took the pan from the range. "Can't say I was surprised, either. She tried to make light of it, saying there wasn't much time on Sunday for you to have told her. And then Bertha had to go and blab that you'd taken Nan down to Ben's place and how Nan would step right in and take charge if you said the word."

"Oh, Mam, 'tis not fair putting it all on me," Bertha protested. "You went on about how Nan would make Alan a good wife and singing her praises . . ."

"I'll not deny it, but 'twas done for a purpose. I wanted to see how Jenny would take that sort of talk."

There was a heavy silence, and then Alan asked, "And how did she take it?"

"She went very quiet, and made a mess of the scone she was eating. Then she said she must be going. As she was leaving, she said to tell you how glad she was for you, about getting the farm. You'm a grown man now, as you keep telling me, Alan, and I suppose you know what you're about but I wish you'd let me know just which girl I'm supposed to look on as my future daughter-in-law."

"Mother, you know very well . . ."

"I don't know anything, son, except that 'twas but a short while back you told me you loved Jennifer Haslam and always would, and now 'twould seem 'tis Nan Webber that's been down at your future home, acting as if 'twas her own."

"That's nothing to do with me!" he retorted, thumping the table. "I didn't ask Nan to do any cleaning. If she has, then she's interfering where she has no right. And I'll damn well tell her so, *now*." He picked up his coat and strode to the door.

"Alan, your supper."

"To hell with my supper!" He went out, slamming the door behind him.

But it was not to Nan's home that he rode. When

he came to the fork in the road he suddenly realized that far more important than putting Nan Webber in her place was to straighten things out with Jenny. Riding down the hill to Wellsworthy, his mother's words kept repeating themselves in his head:

She went very quiet.

He knew what that meant. When Jenny went quiet, she was either deeply moved or deeply hurt. He knew her so well, better than anybody else did, except perhaps Mollie. Every change of mood, every inflection of her voice, each gesture; all had been clearly imprinted on his mind during the years of knowing her, loving her. And what did that damned American know about her? All *he* would see would be her "London" self. And how long would Jenny's interest in *him* last? Surely she would have the sense to see Darrell Meares for what he was, a man with too much money, ruthless beneath the charm and good looks, a man with a biting tongue and a foul temper. But with another side, she had said, a kinder side. But then, she *would* say that, being Jenny, always ready to make allowances, and with her gift for friendship, for loving. He felt a little embarrassed at the word and yet he knew it to be true, for Jenny did love people, all kinds of people, ranging from Lady Cleave with her foibles and eccentricities to Ned Hext the wall-builder with his idealistic poetry and earthy stories. In their turn they bore her a deep affection and her absence these last two years had made a gap in their lives.

But to the American, Alan thought, Lady Cleave would seem just a stupid old woman fussing about some unproductive plant he'd done away with, and Ned Hext merely a labourer he might wish to employ to help build the walls around all those hundreds of acres he'd acquired at the stroke of a pen.

And how long will Darrell Meares last on the moor, anyway? He'd retreated to Torquay last winter, and at the first hint of snow it was likely he'd be off again. That should decide Jenny against him, if nothing else did, Alan thought with satisfaction. She would have to be head-over-heels in love with a man to face the prospect of being parted from her beloved Dartmoor, now that she had come back to it again after two years of "exile" as she'd termed it.

He had reached the bend in the river when he saw her. She was standing on the footbridge, facing upstream away from him. Her lemon-coloured dress was dappled with shadows cast by the rowan trees and the last of the sunlight shone on her smooth dark hair. It was how he had first seen her, only she had been a little girl then, just like the painting in the parlour at Lidden Barton. Looking back afterwards, it had seemed to him that, young as he was, he had known then that this would be the one girl he would ever want as his wife. At that time it had been just a foolish notion for he was the son of a moorland farmer, gauche and tongue-tied, and she a professor's daughter, knowledgeable about so many things and completely self-assured.

She did not look self-assured now, he saw as he drew nearer. Her shoulders drooped and she was listlessly snapping off dead twigs from a branch of scrub oak and dropping them into the river.

Alan dismounted and tethered his pony and scrambled over the litter of boulders and twisted roots. The river was running high, the ripple and gurgle of rushing water covering the sound of his approach so that when he touched her hand and spoke her name, she turned with a start. And then, to his relief, he saw pleasure light up her face, her lips part in a smile of welcome.

He said, "I came as soon as I could. I've been . . ."

"Yes, your mother told me. Did the cattle fetch a good price?"

"The cattle?" he repeated, not understanding.

"The ones you and your father took down to the in-country."

"Oh, that," he said dismissively. "I meant, I came as soon as I heard from mother that you were upset because I hadn't told you about Stadden."

She turned away and he saw her hand tighten on the rail of the bridge. "It was foolish of me," she said, having to raise her voice above the sound of the river. "It's your affair, Alan, if you want Nan Webber . . ."

"I don't want Nan, not in any way at all. And she has nothing what ever to do with Stadden."

Jennifer swung back to face him and two red

spots appeared in her cheeks. "Alan, don't lie to me. Bertha said that you had taken Nan down to see Ben's place and when I—when I decided just to ride down and have a look at it on my way home, Nan was there, acting as if she were already mistress of the place."

"I didn't know she was going down there, Jenny, honestly."

"That's what she told me," Jenny admitted. "She said it was to be a surprise and that you would be delighted."

"Well, I'm not," he said fiercely, "and I shall tell her so in no uncertain terms. And neither did I take her down and show her the place, that was entirely Bertha's imagination."

He saw doubt come into her eyes, then she said, "But you *had* told Nan that you'd been successful in getting the lease?"

"Yes, I did mention it, but . . ." He caught hold of her hands. "Jenny, please listen to me. Perhaps I've been a fool but—well, I was jealous, and when I learned you were with Mr Meares . . ."

"What *are* you talking about?"

So then he told her, how he had ridden back from Princetown in such high spirits, his one thought to tell *her*, before anybody else, of his success; how he had bounded up the steps of Lidden Barton only to be met with the news that she was dining at Heronslea; how, like a fool, he had asked Mrs Westcott not to mention his visit.

"I meant to tell you about Stadden on Sunday," he went on as he saw how dumbfounded she looked, "but then, the first thing I saw was Mr Meares' carriage . . ."

"But, Alan, you knew I wasn't expecting him and anyway, he was just about to leave when all that fuss with your cart and his carriage erupted. Surely you saw how furious I was with him, and I *did* praise you for the way you handled the situation."

"Yes, I can see that now," he admitted, feeling ashamed. "But by that time I was just damnably jealous."

"Because I'd gone—with Papa, please remember —to Heronslea?"

"No. It started before that, actually on the evening Mr Meares and I arrived at your home at the same time."

He saw that she was thinking back to that evening. "But Papa took Mr Meares into his study, don't you remember? It was you I talked to that evening, not him."

"That's not quite true, Jenny, is it? You told me you were very tired and so I left you, although there was still a great deal I wanted to say. Then, just as I was opening the gate to the meadow, I saw the American come into the parlour and you smiled at him and then he took hold of your hands and—and . . . It was a wonder I ever reached home that night."

"Why? Whatever do you mean by that?"

"I didn't care whether I broke my pony's neck or my own."

She said uncertainly, "Alan, I've never known you talk like this. I hadn't realized . . ."

"No, I don't suppose you have. Because I've seen that it will take you a little while to adjust again to this kind of life and because you had the shock of finding Hannah Sculpher and—oh, for several other reasons, I've . . ."

"Yes?" she prompted as he came to a stop.

He let go of her hands and gripped the wooden rail, watching the turbulent water gushing and frothing its way around the granite boulders, while he sought for the right words.

"I've curbed my real feelings," he said at last, "but it doesn't mean that they aren't . . . What I'm trying to say is, we're not boy and girl any longer, Jenny, and I want you . . . I want you so much that there are times when I can't think of anything else. I'm not putting this very well, but surely you understand that it's part of my loving you, and so is being jealous. If I thought that there was any hope that you could feel—the same way . . ."

He came to a stop, realizing that she was not giving him the slightest encouragement. She had started dropping twigs into the water again and her face was troubled.

"I see," he said heavily. "Is it the American?"

She looked at him and to his surprise she seemed near to tears, and her voice was shaky as she said,

"Alan, I don't know, I truly don't know. And how can I explain it to you when I don't understand my own feelings? I dislike everything Mr Meares stands for and I've involved myself in the fight against him, and yet, now that I feel sorry for him and . . ."

"*Sorry* for him?"

"He—he has had a great personal tragedy in his life, and he *is* lonely."

"I see," he said again, but with bitterness this time. "So that's the way to win a woman—make her feel sorry for you. In that case, I've certainly no chance. I'd never ask you to be sorry for *me*, whatever . . ."

"You seem to forget," she said, her voice suddenly sharp, "that's just what you did, when you thought you couldn't apply for Stadden because of your suspicions about your mother. *And* I responded, if you remember, by riding at once to Hannah Sculpher's, and despite the shock I had there, almost my first thought was to let you know that Ben's death couldn't possibly have been caused by Hannah's witchcraft. And that's how you came to get Stadden," she ended with what sounded very like triumph in her voice.

He was completely bowled over. And then, suddenly, he saw the funny side. He started to laugh. Jenny stared at him in astonishment. Then she, too, was laughing. They took hold of one another's hands and kissed each other lightly, as in the past, and Jennifer said:

"You are a darling, Alan, and I do love you, but whether . . . Please, please give me time. I'm all mixed up at present, and so, you see, I can't . . ."

He took her face between his hands. "I understand. The last thing I want, Jenny, is for you to make the wrong decision. I'd rather live the rest of my life alone than make you unhappy."

It had rained heavily again during the night and the moor was running with water as Jennifer set out next day to visit her grandfather. In the ordinary way she would have left the turnpike road and cut up across the moor towards Cock Tor, stopping on the far side to have a chat with Mollie's father, then continued down into the valley of the Dart and up again to bring her out near the stone quarry where her grandfather had been foreman. Now the wall of Darrell Meares' enclosure barred her way and she had to make a detour. Halfway up the hill she came upon Ned Hext, trudging happily along, his clay pipe jutting from his mouth.

"Good morning, Ned," she greeted him cheerfully. "Are you having a day off?"

He grinned at her. "You do know I never take a day off, 'cept Sundays. And I've a long walk afore I reach my work today for I'm on my way to Stadden to build the newtake walls for Alan Vicary. 'Twill be a nice little farm, that, when he's got it into shape. Mind you, I do reckon some of his ideas to be a bit far-fetched, but then, I'm getting on in years and he'm a young man set on getting ahead. One thing you can be sure of, he'll want them walls built properly, and he'd know if they weren't—not like this 'foreigner' " he added scornfully. "Still, I'd best keep such thoughts to myself by all accounts."

"Why?"

He regarded her thoughtfully. "You'm proper friendly with the American gentleman, so I've heard tell, and after what he've had done upalong I don't reckon you'll want to hear anything agin him."

"I don't understand," she said, puzzled.

"Haven't 'ee seen, then?"

"Seen what?"

"That little combe you'm so fond of—ah, you didn't know I knew about that did 'ee, but there's not much misses old Ned, m'dear, going around quiet like to watch the wild creatures as I do. I've seen you go there secretly, saw you down there the day your mother died and thought of offering a word of comfort, but then I reckoned that 'twas why you'd gone there, to be on your lonesome."

She was dumbfounded, but grateful, too. "You're very understanding. Thank you. But what did you mean, had I seen the combe? It's within the Heronslea enclosure, as you must know."

"Not any longer. The American had every man jack of them working like niggers up there, taking down the wall and rebuilding it quarter of a mile back, and they brought in a team of oxen to drag a gurt granite slab to form a bridge across the new leat."

At first she could not believe it. "Ned, is this true?" she asked doubtfully. "You're not teasing me?"

"I'd not tease 'ee about a thing like that. Just you ride upalong and see for yourself. I reckon this 'foreigner' has some good in him after all, despite what most folks do say about un."

"Yes, he has," Jennifer said. "If only he could be made to see . . ."

"Other folks' views? The moormen's views, in fact? But they do go agin those of the miners he'm employing *and* the folks that'll do well out of his timber when 'tis ready for felling. 'Tis always the same, Miss Jenny, and always will be, seems to me. What does one man good does another one harm. 'Tis the way of the world, and since the world was ordained by God according to parson's teaching, I reckon there be little us can do about it."

"But the moormen are my—our people," she said earnestly. "They belong here, as you and I do. The tin miners . . ."

"There've been tin miners on the moor from a long time back, and they be men with wives and childer, same as any other."

"Then—then you don't think anyone should attempt to alter what's been done—to try and get back the commoners' rights, I mean?"

He sucked hard on his pipe. "I don't reckon what

I think will make a mite of difference. Men born on the granite don't give in easy, and some of them are prepared . . . Well, never mind about that, 'tis not for you to worry your pretty head over such things."

"But I do worry, Ned. The people who have been wronged are my friends. Are you suggesting they will do something drastic—violent? If so, they should be stopped. There are other ways of putting things right, peaceful ways in which there would be no risk of anybody getting hurt. Ned, if you hear of any dangerous plans, please try to stop them."

He took his pipe from his mouth and gazed at it intently. Then he looked up at her. "Would you be asking that for their sake, Miss Jenny, or for Mr Meares'?"

"For theirs, of course," she answered at once. "They haven't a hope, not against a man like Mr Meares. He's used to employing hundreds of . . ."

"Negro slaves, were you going to say?" he asked as she hesitated. "But moormen aren't slaves, Miss Jenny, and they'll not be kept down like those poor niggers, or knuckle under without a fight." He shifted his pack more firmly on his shoulders. "I reckon I'll make a poem about it one day. 'Twill be like the war of American independence back in the last century, only this time 'twill be a few British fighting for *their* independence against one American."

"I do hope you're not right," she said anxiously as they parted, and added to herself, "For my own sake as well as everybody else's. Because, if there should be a fight of any kind, I shall find myself right in the middle."

She was so worried about what might happen that it filled her mind to the exclusion of the news Ned had given her about Darrell excluding "her" combe from his enclosure. She was still wondering whether there was any way in which she could tell Darrell that there was likely to be an enquiry into his legal right to acquire so much land, without spoiling the new relationship which had sprung up between them after his disclosure of his personal tragedy, when she reached her grandfather's home.

But within five minutes of her arrival she forgot her own problems. The old man was in bed with bronchitis and Aunt Sarah was struggling to carry out the day's work while suffering from a severe migraine headache. Jennifer sent her upstairs to lie down, changed her riding habit for an old dress of her aunt's, rolled up her sleeves, tucked the skirt into the waistband and set to work. There were two goats to be milked, hens to be fed and eggs collected, peat to be fetched from the stack in the yard and the fire made up. She baked a batch of bread and made some tarts, filling them with whortleberries and blackberries she found in a basin in the larder. Then she took up some chicken broth to her grandfather and stayed to talk to him for a while. After her own light meal, she scrubbed the kitchen table and floor and polished the dresser and chairs, and the horse brasses fastened to the lintel of the fireplace.

"And how I wish Nan Webber could see *this*," she thought, triumphantly surveying the result of her work.

By early evening Aunt Sarah was much better, although feeling washed out, as always after such an attack.

"I can't tell you how grateful I am," she said, as Jennifer was preparing to leave. "You've been an absolute godsend and no mistake. But I'm sorry that you should have been faced with this, on your first visit here after coming back from London. And I did so want to hear all about your doings up there."

"Next time," Jennifer promised. "And as for helping out today, I've enjoyed it. After all the time-wasting in London, it's good to be doing something really useful. Will you be able to manage tomorrow or shall I come over again?"

"I'll be fine now, Jenny dear, and I'll be able to take it easy after all you've done today."

Jennifer was tired, but satisfied, as she rode homewards, keeping Bracken to a walk at first so that she could enjoy the view. The sun was setting in splendour over the Cornish hills, its last rays lighting up the raindrops on heather and gorse and bracken, for there had been a shower just before she set out. She felt as if she were riding through a land spread with precious jewels. She had only the moorland ponies for company because most of the agistered cattle and sheep had been taken down to their owners whose farms lay in the milder, softer land of the "in-country". A buzzard mewed far overhead and a lark flew up from the ground ahead of her with a quick, short burst of song. Then the sun went down and the moor looked bleak and sombre.

Bracken needed no urging to quicken her pace along the ridge of hills. They descended into a wide combe, forded a stream and climbed up the other side. And then, with the suddenness so typical of Dartmoor, they were into mist. It swirled and eddied all about them, damp and chill, and at this time of day, even to Jennifer a little frightening.

She changed direction, following a track which ran alongside a stream, knowing it would lead her eventually to the turnpike road. She did not dare give the mare her head, for she might very well make for her former home at Edgecombe Farm instead of Lidden Barton.

When they reached the road, she knew she had nothing to worry about, provided she kept the verge in sight. Even so, it took all her concentration. The mist would lift for a moment, revealing the sodden grass, only to close in the next, blotting out everything at ground level except Bracken's hooves. At one point it cleared sufficiently for her to see the newly-built wall of the Heronslea enclosure on her left.

It was just afterwards that she heard voices. She was glad. Used as she was to a moorland mist, the feeling of being alone in a cold grey world was not one she relished.

Then, abruptly, she reined in. The voices, even though they were low-pitched, sounded angry, as if several men were having a quarrel. She hoped they were going in the opposite direction, suspecting that they were some of the miners who had found employment at Heronslea and who had earned a reputation for roughness and drunkenness. But she could not hear any footsteps, only the voices coming out of the mist. Then she made out a sentence or two, as one of the men spoke more loudly and angrily than the others.

"Mist'll serve us well . . . wreck the whole plantation . . . what he deserves . . . like to burn his bliddy house down *and* him in it."

Jennifer felt cold all over and her heart began to pound. Her immediate reaction was to ride away from whatever was about to happen at Heronslea as fast as she could. She tried to turn Bracken but the mare would have none of it, sensing that she was nearing her warm stable.

A figure came out of the mist, calling, "Who's there?"

Jennifer could have laughed aloud with relief. The man was Mollie's father.

But instead of greeting her in his usual friendly way, he asked sharply, "How long you been here?"

"Only a few minutes. I heard voices and . . ."

"Did you hear what was being said?"

"I . . ." She hesitated, made anxious by the way he was looking at her. "Only a few words . . . It sounded like a quarrel. I thought I'd come on some of the rough miners and I was—frightened."

"So what were you going to do?"

"I was trying to turn my pony, I was . . ."

Again she came to a halt, alarmed by the suspicion in his eyes. The other men were holding back and were hidden by the mist but she was very much aware of them, listening to what was being said.

Mollie's father said, "And how did 'ee think you were going to get home, by any other way than the bridge, in a mist as thick as this un?"

"I—I didn't think. I told you, I acted . . ."

He took hold of her reins and looked closely at her. Lowering his voice, he asked, "Can I be sure you weren't turning back in order to go to Heronslea, to warn that damned 'foreigner' . . .?"

"Of course I wasn't! That's the truth. You *must* believe me."

His manner changed then and he said in his usual kindly voice, "Look'ee, Jenny, you've always been a good friend to my Mollie and she's been telling me you've been wanting to do something to help those of us the American has harmed. But at the same time, we all know you'm mighty friendly with him. Whatever you heard just now, best forget it."

"No!" she exclaimed, no longer afraid. "No, I

can't. Because I must warn you, as I've already warned Ned Hext, that this is not the way to defeat Mr Meares. I've seen how harsh he can be, when he chased poor Zebedee. But he has a kinder side, and if you will only leave it to me . . ."

"To *you?* Do 'ee really expect us . . . ?"

She put a hand on his arm, shaking it in her desire to make him agree. "Give me just a few days. Please. Even if *I* don't succeed, someone else may do so. But not by using violence. That way, it would be the commoners who would suffer, not Darrell Meares."

He was silent for a few moments. Then he said, "Wait here, while I talk this over with the others."

She could hear their low voices coming out of the mist. Bracken grew impatient, tossing her head and pawing the ground. Then Jennifer heard another sound, men's footsteps, growing fainter and fainter.

Mollie's father came to her. "I've persuaded them," he said, "but they'll only hold off for a few days, Jenny, and they don't altogether trust you."

"Then please assure them," she said firmly, "that if they see me going to Heronslea tomorrow, it will be on *their* behalf, and as soon as I learn anything definite I will ride up to the warren and tell you."

Darrell was reading a newspaper over a late breakfast. It contained disturbing news about the situation in America. The abolitionists in the North were pressing their cause and the Southern planters were

talking of seceding from the union. He was thoughtful as he drank his coffee, seeing in his mind's eye
not the cold, heather-clad uplands of Dartmoor, but
the level stretches of the cotton and sugar planta-
tions, and the vast tobacco lands of Virginia. It was
both absurd and dangerous to talk about freeing all
slaves. Absurd because the whole economy of most
of the Southern states depended on slave labour.
Besides, if they were freed, where would they go,
where else would they find employment, shelter,
food? Dangerous because the blacks outnumbered
the whites and since many of them had not been
long out of the jungle, they must be kept under
strict control.

Darrell tried to close his mind to such thoughts,
as he had tried to close it to memories of his family.
South Carolina was not for him, not any longer.
And yet, if the quarrel should develop, become as
grave and threatening as was being hinted, was not
his place there amongst his own kind?

Impatiently he pushed his cup away and rose,
scraping his chair on the polished wood floor. Then,
abruptly, his thoughts were diverted, for Jacob came
into the dining-room to announce:

"Miss Haslam is here to see you, suh."

Darrell was about to go to her at once, then
changed his mind. "Show her into the drawing-
room. I will join her shortly."

All the previous day he had expected her. From
his bedroom window he had seen her, riding up the

hill beyond the enclosure wall, stopping to talk to some old man with a pack on his back. When she rode on again she was heading towards the place she had told him about, her special place which he had now freed from the enclosure so that she could go there in peace. Except as an added source of water it had been of little use to him but including it had kept the line of the wall straight and his eye was offended by the irregular curve. Later, when she became his wife, he could have the wall rebuilt on its original course but a man had to make some concessions if he wanted to win a woman, especially a young woman with such definite views as Jennifer Haslam.

He had hung about all yesterday morning, expecting her to come as soon as she had seen what he had done for her. He had gone out in the afternoon and been more disappointed then he cared to admit when, on his return, he found she still had not called at Heronslea.

If she chose to be tardy in expressing her gratitude, she could be kept waiting, too. He paced up and down the dining-room, pausing to investigate a smear on the highly polished surface of the table, running his finger along the sideboard to see if it had been properly dusted. When he saw by the French clock on the mantelpiece that ten minutes had passed, he went leisurely across the hall and into the drawing-room.

Jennifer was standing by the window, leaning forward to look at something outside which had caught her attention. She appeared very small and youthful in her blue riding-habit with the frivolous little hat perched at an angle on her dark hair. For a moment he was reminded of his sister, Susanna, and, from force of habit, thrust the memory quickly aside. Then, recalling what Jennifer had advised, he deliberately allowed the thought back into his mind. It was not going to be easy, for he had closed the door on memories of happy times for so long, recalling, in nightmares and moments of despair, only those moments of tragedy which had changed his life.

"Good morning, Mr Meares," Jennifer said, coming towards him. "I'm so sorry I wasn't able to call on you yesterday. I went to visit my grandfather and when I arrived I found he was very unwell and that my Aunt Sarah had a migraine headache. So I had to stay for the whole day, cooking and cleaning and milking the goats and . . . Why are you looking at me so disapprovingly? Don't you like goats?"

"I have no knowledge of them, Miss Haslam, and I had not intended to appear disapproving. I was merely surprised to learn that you . . ."

"Knew how to milk? I learned that very early in life. But I *was* rather out of practice and I don't think the goats enjoyed it much."

She was laughing, and he smiled too, but he was thinking that there would be no more playing at milkmaids once she was mistress of Heronslea.

"It *was* kind of you," she went on, "to alter the line of the wall so that 'my' little combe is outside your enclosure, and to put a bridge across the leat. I wish . . ."

"Well?" he prompted as she hesitated.

She did not answer at once. She was playing with her whip, running the thong between her gloved fingers. Then she looked up at him, her eyes troubled.

"I wish you would show this—this side of your character to other people. You can be so considerate, and yet . . ."

"What *other* people?" he asked coldly, and saw the uncertainty deepen in her eyes.

Damn all women, he thought, why couldn't they be satisfied with what they were given, instead of forever wanting more? He had made two concessions already. He had told her about his family and he had freed those few acres of moorland which seemed so important to her.

She turned away, and let the end of her whip trail along the carpet. "It's no use, is it? Nothing I say will make any difference. I just hoped there could be some—some sort of compromise."

"I am not used to making compromises, Miss Haslam, and I am afraid that if you thought to persuade me to forego my plans merely to gratify the whims of . . ."

"I'm not talking about whims," she broke in, "but about people's living, about the difference between men being able to support their families through a hard winter or . . ."

"Would you not agree that is what *I* have done for the tin miners who were thrown out of work?"

"Yes, I grant you that. But the work you've given them is only temporary. When the walls are built, your planting done, the building completed, you will dismiss those men. But the moormen will still be here, finding it harder and harder to live."

"Without a few dozen rabbits, or a basinful of whortleberries?" he asked sarcastically. "If that is the way these 'friends' of yours exist, then it is high time they changed their way of life and sought some more profitable occupation."

She stood quite still, the whip trailing at her side, looking up at him with an expression he found difficult to interpret. Then she said slowly. "If there is no bread, let them eat cake."

"I beg your pardon?"

"It is what Marie Antoinette is reputed to have said when the starving people rioted before the Palace of Versailles."

"Are you suggesting . . . ?"

"I am suggesting that your attitude is in a way akin to hers, and that you have almost as little understanding."

He stared at her, wondering if she really meant him to take her seriously. No woman, nor even any man, had ever spoken to him in such a manner. For the sake of his self-esteem he decided to make light of her words.

He said jocularly, "I seem to recall that the French queen had her head cut off. I trust you are not anticipating . . ."

"No, nothing so drastic." Her tone was sharp and he realized, with growing dismay, that she was in fact deadly serious. "I do, however, anticipate trouble. If it comes I hope you will remember that for—for your sake as well as for that of my friends —the people you so despise—I have done my best to prevent it. And now, I had better leave."

As she made for the door, he barred her way. "What game do you think you're playing?" he demanded, unable to accept her warning.

"It's not a game, Mr Meares, I assure you. When I came here this morning, I felt towards you some degree of . . . That is, I had hoped the kindness you had shown me, and the fact that you had confided in me the sorrow you had endured, might mean that . . ."

"That I could be twisted round your little finger so that I would give in to this bunch of ignorant yokels?" he said angrily. "You little fool, don't you understand the first thing about men? I told you about my family, and I freed that damned gully, for one reason only—because I wanted you, as a *woman,* not as a sanctimonious, preaching little . . ."

He saw the colour rush into her cheeks, her eyes widen with shock and anger, and he saw her also as utterly desirable. As she tried to step past him, he caught hold of her. Pressing her hard against his body, he kissed her roughly, bruising her mouth.

She struggled fiercely but she was only a little thing and no match for him and the more she struggled the stronger grew his desire to possess and master her. She tried to kick his shins and he laughed because her efforts were so futile. For a moment he loosed his hold on her. It was enough for her to free her right hand. She thrust the butt of her whip upwards, so that it caught him beneath his jaw. There was a loud click as his teeth clamped together. Gasping with mingled shock and pain, he released her and reeled backwards. She raised her arm and struck him full across the face with the leather thong. Then she ran for the door, wrenched it open and was out in the hall before he could stop her.

He heard Jacob's startled exclamation, the opening of the front door, her footsteps as she hurried down the steps, and then the thud of hooves on gravel. Jacob was standing in the hall, eyes wide, mouth open in astonishment.

For one blinding moment Darrell was tempted to vent his anger on the Negro. Then, suddenly he began to laugh. Was not the girl's behaviour exactly as he would have wished? There was no satisfaction in possessing a woman who was pliant and yielding and who put up no resistance. He would master Jennifer Haslam in the end, no doubt of that, and he was going to derive a great deal of pleasure in doing so. It might be as well to make some further small concession, though, give back a few of those idiotic rabbit burrows or let one of the moormen on to his land for an hour or two to cut peat for winter fuel. The months ahead, he thought with relish, were certainly not going to be dull.

"What the hell are you standing there for, Jacob?" he demanded. "Haven't you work to do?"

"I just thought, suh . . ."

"I don't pay you to think, but to . . ."

Through the open front door Darrell heard the sound of a carriage drawing up before the steps.

"Who the devil can that be?"

"I will go and see, suh," the Negro answered with dignity, "as that is what I *am* paid for."

Darrell went to the window. His jaw was still painful and his cheek bleeding a little. He dabbed at it with his handkerchief while he took a look at the carriage. There was a coat of arms on the door panel, a footman as well as a coachman, both of them dressed in green and yellow livery. Between the shafts were two beautifully matched greys.

Jacob returned, carrying a visiting card.

Sir Robert Bratton, Bt., Q.C., Darrell read.

His visitor must be one of the local gentry, Darrell decided, paying a social call. *That* made a change.

"Show Sir Robert in," Darrell told Jacob as he went back into the drawing-room. He saw the butler's eyebrows lift and knew exactly what Jacob was thinking: How can you receive an English gentleman in the condition you are in at the moment?

As his visitor, a middle-aged, imposing looking man dressed formally in black frock coat and dark trousers, came into the room, Darrell bowed and said composedly, "I trust you will forgive my appearance, sir. I—I had the misfortune to slip as I was coming downstairs."

Sir Robert gave him a frosty smile which hid, Darrell felt sure, disbelief in his explanation. He said suavely, "I trust you have sustained no lasting injury?"

"No, it's nothing but a slight cut on the cheek and a bruised jaw. It is civil of you to call. May I offer you some wine?"

"Thank you, but I will not take any refreshment. I have been calling on my cousin and she always insists that I sample her latest home-made wine. I found this one somewhat of a heady brew."

"Your cousin?" Darrell said conversationally.

"Lady Cleave. I believe you met her, briefly, at Professor Haslam's house last Sunday."

For a moment Darrell could not recall the name. Then he remembered the eccentric old woman who had complained that he had destroyed some plant she wanted preserved. He was reminded also, with some embarrassment, that she had been a witness to his exhibition of bad temper.

Feeling his way, he said, "I did have that pleasure. She was not very pleased with me, I recollect, because I had unwittingly destroyed a rare botanical specimen."

"Yes, well, we all have our foibles," the older man said, with the same frosty smile. "Although my cousin *is* concerned in the matter about which I called to see you, it has nothing to do with rare plants."

So this was not a mere social call after all, Darrell thought, and glanced at the card he was still holding. He saw that his visitor was not only a baronet but also a barrister. And certainly, although his manner was perfectly polite, it was by no means cordial.

"Lawyers have a reputation for prevarication," Sir Robert said, sitting back in his chair and crossing one leg over the other, "but I prefer to come straight to the point. I am fortunate enough to have a private income and therefore the only briefs I accept nowadays are ones which really interest me. This has the added advantage of leaving me free at other times to indulge in *my* foibles."

"You are indeed fortunate," Darrell said, wondering where this was leading.

"You also, Mr Meares, I would imagine, are in much the same position. You are a gentleman of some considerable means, I understand, and so this scheme to establish a plantation of trees and to grow flax and hemp—which has little hope of success . . ."

"May I ask why you think that?" Darrell interrupted.

"Because such ventures have been attempted previously on the moor. Sir Thomas Tyrwhitt, for instance, had high hopes and the best of intentions but Dartmoor is no respecter of persons or hopes. The climate, the soil, the very granite itself, are all against the type of development which is practised elsewhere. It takes a man born on these uplands, who has learned their limitations, to make a success of . . ."

"*I* intend to make a success of what I have undertaken," Darrell declared, his irritation increased by the soreness of his jaw and cheek. "Forgive me, sir, but you did say you were coming straight to the point."

"Yes, you are right. I was just wondering if, before I did so, I had any chance of persuading you to . . ."

"Give up?" Darrell stood with his hands clenched by his sides. "No, by God, I will not. I've already had one visitor this morning who made it very plain that I was not popular amongst the local population, but . . ."

"The young lady who almost collided with my carriage in your drive?" the lawyer asked, unmoved by Darrell's anger. "She seemed somewhat—distressed, I thought."

"I don't care a fig what you thought! Neither you, nor your cousin fussing about some stupid plant, nor these ignorant peasants who live from hand to mouth because they . . ."

His visitor was on his feet now, but his suave manner had not changed, and his voice was controlled and quiet as he said:

"I deeply regret that you have taken this attitude, sir. It means, you see, that other and more forceful methods will have to be employed. I refer, as you would expect, to the law."

Darrell stared at him, in blank astonishment. "What the devil do you mean by that?"

"As I was remarking just now, we all have our foibles, for want of a better word. One of mine is to study old documents, legal documents, you understand. They sometimes prove very fascinating, especially those relating to the rights which were granted to commoners and to those people who held land by tenure of copyhold, in return for certain services. What emerges, especially on Dartmoor, is that these rights have been gradually eroded, sometimes by farmers seeking to increase their acreage, at other times by newcomers who have obtained leases from lawyers who have had no real right to grant them, or even from the Duchy of Cornwall's agents who have not always gone sufficiently carefully into the matter. The position, naturally, is a delicate one, since we are dealing with the Crown property. I think you should know, however, that in my opinion, the lease granted to you to enclose so much of what for generations has been common land, is entirely illegal."

Scarcely able to believe his ears, Darrell said rudely, "You're talking nonsense! It was signed and witnessed, and bears a seal . . ."

"I've no doubt of it. But then, so have a number of documents which have subsequently been proved in a court of law . . ."

Darrell stepped forward. "Are you threatening me?"

"That is not a word I care for, Mr Meares. I am merely informing you that if I were asked to accept a brief to contest your right to the land you have enclosed, I should most readily accept it, and without any payment whatsoever. I suggest you think that over, sir, very carefully. And now, good-day."

Darrell did not move as Sir Robert walked to the door. Then, as his visitor paused in the hall for Jacob to bring his hat and gloves, Darrell joined him and said angrily:

"You don't think all that talk about an interest in old documents fooled me, do you? Somebody has put you up to this, somebody who has reason to . . . Ah, yes, your cousin. You said she was concerned in the affair."

"Certainly she is," the lawyer agreed evenly, "but she is by no means the only one."

"My God!" Darrell exclaimed, suddenly seeing the truth. "This is Jennifer Haslam's doing, isn't it? She spoke about warning me, about anticipating trouble, about . . . If she thinks I'm going to be beaten by a slip of a girl who spends half her time milking goats and—and hobnobbing with yokels, she's very much mistaken. I'll fight her, and I'll fight you, Sir Robert, and anyone else who sets himself up against me."

But the barrister was half-way down the steps and his footman stepping forward to open the carriage door. As the coachman gathered up the reins and the splendid greys moved off down the drive, Darrell turned to find Jacob beside him.

"If there is fighting to be done," the Negro said reproachfully, "why do you not return and do it in your own country—our country? You tell me there is trouble in America, the North turning against the South, and that it will become worse. So that's where you ought to be, Massa Darrell, with your own people. Why do you stay here, where you are not wanted, when there is need of you at home?"

"Damn you, Jacob, hold your tongue!" Darrell shouted. "And tell that incompetent fool of a groom to saddle my horse—at once."

Jacob looked worried. "You sure you ought to go riding, suh? I think it would be better if . . ."

"I don't want to hear what you think. Just carry out my orders."

The Negro put a hand on Darrell's arm. "You mind you don't break your neck."

"If I did, what the devil would it matter? Do you think anyone—anyone at all, would care?"

"I would care, and Miss Haslam, too, I believe, and all the people at home who . . ."

"*This* is my home now. How many times do I have to repeat that?"

"You can repeat it a hundred times, Massa Darrell," Jacob said calmly, "but you would not make me believe it. And you do not truly believe it yourself. And that is where the true fight is, within yourself."

"Damn you, Jacob!" Darrell swore again, wrenching his arm free. "Do as I ordered and tell that groom to have my horse saddled—in five minutes, or it will be the worse for both of you."

He went swiftly upstairs and changed into riding breeches. Ten minutes later he was mounted on the chestnut, turning his back on Heronslea and its enclosures, trying to shut out from his mind that scene with Jennifer Haslam and the carefully worded threat from Sir Robert Bratton. What he could not shut out were Jacob's words, and the unpalatable truth, which he did not want to admit, that Jacob, and Jennifer Haslam, too, for that matter, were right.

Chapter Seven

Jennifer reined in just beyond the gates of Herons-lea. She was trembling and her heart thudding painfully. Only Bracken's swift leap on to the bank had saved them both from disaster as a carriage swung into the drive.

Even in that moment of danger she had seen a coat of arms on the door panel, and at the window the startled face of a man wearing a top hat. She had not met Sir Robert Bratton but she had no doubt that it was he who was about to call on Darrell Meares. An hour ago, she would have wished to prevent that meeting, still hoping as she had been, that she could persuade the American to make some concessions. Instead, had it not been for that near-collision, she would have stopped the carriage and urged the barrister to do all in his power to bring Darrell to his knees.

Dismounting, she put her arms around Bracken's neck and leant her cheek against the mare's soft muzzle. She longed to go to her special place where she could have sat under the rowan tree beside the tumbling stream, letting the peace and beauty of the combe bring calm and reassurance. That was impossible now. Even though there was no wall to stop her, there was the invisible barrier of Darrell's association with the place.

So where to go for comfort? If only her mother had still been alive. But then, she thought ruefully, she would not have found herself in such a predicament. Her mother, full of good sense, would have foreseen what would happen, would have warned that if you played with fire you must expect to get burned.

If she went home, Mrs Westcott's sharp eyes would notice at once her bruised lips and dishevelled hair, the torn blouse and the button hanging loosely from her jacket. And she could not face her father in this state.

To Alan, then? Always, in the past, he had been ready to listen to her troubles. But this? No, not this. And Mrs Vicary was not a woman on whose shoulder Jennifer could have a good cry and so rid herself of these shattering, pent-up feelings.

She had to talk to someone. If only she had not parted from Mollie in the middle of what amounted to a quarrel. A quarrel caused, she suddenly realized, by her defence of Darrell Meares and her reluctance to accept her friend's warning that she could not have a foot in both camps. Mollie had been right, she saw now, and Mollie had been a loyal and understanding friend since early childhood.

Jennifer remounted and rode up the hill which overlooked Lidden Barton, then down into the valley, fording the river at the wide bend where the water ran placid and shallow. And so she came to Wellsworthy. Tethering Bracken to an iron ring in the wall of the smithy, she knocked on Mollie's door and waited, instead of opening it and calling a greeting as she had done before. It seemed an age before she heard footsteps. Then Mollie was opening the door, hastily taking off her apron and tidying her hair.

"Why, Jenny, I never thought 'twould be you!" she exclaimed in surprise. "Whyever didn't you . . .? Jenny, whatever's the matter?"

She drew Jennifer inside the cottage and quickly closed the door against the inquisitive eyes of a passing neighbour. Jennifer tried to keep control of herself, to think up some story about having fallen from Bracken, but it was no use. She found herself sitting in a chair beside the fire, with her friend's arms about her, the tears running unchecked down her cheeks.

Mollie said in a shocked voice, "This is a man's doing, isn't it? Alan—surely not Alan?"

Jennifer jerked up her head. "Of *course* not, Alan," she denied fiercely, and as soon as she had spoken those words it was as if a shutter had been lifted from her mind.

She was vaguely aware of Mollie sponging her face, putting salve on her lips, tidying her hair, then bringing her a cup of tea. She knew that Mollie asked questions and that she made some kind of answers. She sat obediently still while Mollie mended the tear in her blouse and stitched the loose button in place. She was grateful for what her friend was doing, and thankful for Mollie's presence but far more important was what was going on in her mind.

Her thoughts now were all centred on Alan. Alan, who had given her the mare she had taken a fancy to two years ago and which would have earned him much-needed money at the October sales; who had borrowed a trap to meet her at Moretonhampstead because she was a "fine London lady" now; who had ridden from Princetown to tell her, first of all, that his dream of acquiring the lease of Stadden had come true, and been consumed with jealousy because of her association with the American; who had remained calm and courteous during that dreadful scene in the driveway of Lidden Barton. Alan who had said:

"I'd rather live the rest of my life alone than make you unhappy."

As she recalled the events since her return from London, she saw something else clearly, too. Despite her attraction to Darrell Meares, her first thought all along had been for Alan, and she in her turn had been jealous, of Nan Webber.

She said, interrupting Mollie's flow of talk, "I've been such a fool."

"Haven't we all?" her friend said comfortably. "And some of us have to endure hard lessons before we come to our senses. You know, Jenny, I think part of your trouble was that you didn't fall in love like those other girls you told me about, while you were in London. If you had, you'd have got it out of your system. Instead, although you were so determined you wanted everything to be the same here, part of you longed for some excitement still, and the American provided it. The fact that you were fighting him at the same time added a bit of zest to the affair."

Jennifer studied her friend's face. "You were right, Mollie, you *have* changed. Being married and having a baby has made you seem not only older but a good deal wiser than I am."

Mollie gave Jennifer's shoulder an affectionate squeeze. "I always was, love," she said cheerfully, "only I took care you didn't realize it. After all, you do have a professor for a father."

They both started to laugh then, and Jennifer felt the last of the tension drain away. When she rose, she knew exactly what she intended to do.

Mollie said, "You don't have to go yet, if you don't want to."

"I do want to, Mollie. I'm—I'm going to Stadden."

"Now? Alan won't be there. He's gone up over after a missing beast. He was down here about an hour ago asking if anyone had seen it."

"I—I don't want Alan to be there. That may sound silly, but I just wish to—to be alone there for a while, and think."

"I hope they're the right kind of thoughts," Mollie said, at the door. "I have a feeling they will be —now."

It was quiet at Stadden, but not depressing as she had found it on her previous visit. The sun was shining, and with a midday warmth unusual for late September. The tinkling of the stream, mingling with the thin song of a robin, were companionable sounds, and a grey wagtail flitted and bobbed amongst the moss-covered boulders near the shallows where the cattle went to drink. Jennifer gathered a handful of blackberries and ate them thoughtfully while she looked around. She could see now with Alan's eyes, visualizing the farmhouse enlarged, the outbuildings repaired and new ones built, a vegetable patch, a flower garden which would be her especial care. Up on the hill, Ned Hext was working on the stone wall which would enclose the newtake, and she could imagine how those extra acres would look, when they had been cleared and ploughed and planted with crops for the cattle's winter feed.

The door, as she expected, was unlocked and she went into the house. It smelt clean and fresh and she shut her mind to the thought that this was Nan's doing. What few possessions Ben had owned were gone now, and in her mind's eye Jennifer was furnishing each room. She could bring some things from Lidden Barton, and for the rest . . .

A hundred guineas, Darrell had said that painting of her as a child would fetch and she believed that in this case, at least, he knew what he was talking about. Alan, with such an independent nature, might prove stubborn at first but if she described the money as a dowry, he could surely not refuse.

There would be difficulties ahead, it was no use pretending otherwise, far more for her to contend with than for Alan. She would still be living between two worlds, her father's and that of Alan's family, and she would have to adjust to that change as well as to marriage. She felt a little daunted as she considered the problems. And then, as she saw the sunshine glinting on the stream and lighting to brilliant gold the gorse bushes on the opposite hill, her spirits rose, and she felt akin to the lark which sprang from a clump of heather and went singing up into the blue sky.

Not for her the time-wasting life she had known in London or the easy life of mistress of Heronslea, even had she truly loved its owner. She needed a challenge, just as Alan did. They would meet this one together. At that thought, she experienced a deep uplifting sense of joy and contentment which put an end to her muddled thoughts and indecision.

And part of this new calmness was the fact that she felt no desire to seek out Alan at once. She knew exactly when she would tell him, drawing him aside after they had stood together at their godson's christening.

As she mounted Bracken and rode away from Stadden she heard shouting. Looking towards the sound, she saw several men disappearing hurriedly over the ridge, carrying ropes and a ladder. She could not imagine what they were about. Out on the road, a village lad ran past and she called:

"What's happening? What's all the fuss about?"

He paused, panting. "The American's horse . . . in . . . Foxtor mire."

"Oh, no! Not that beautiful chestnut?"

"Bliddy vule forced un into it. He'm the same as all 'foreigners', won't be told, think they know everything."

"What about Mr Meares himself?"

"Oh, he'm all right—luck of the devil, he had, seemingly, but Alan . . ."

"*Alan?*" Her heart sank like a pebble in the river. Alan Vicary, do you mean?"

"Who else? Do 'ee know any other man vule enough to go into the mire after a horse?"

She grabbed him by the shoulder as he made to move off. "Are you saying that Alan has actually gone into Foxtor mire to try and save . . . ?"

"Ees, that's right. And 'tis being said he'm under the horse and they can't get un out."

She used heels and whip to urge Bracken to her fastest speed up over the ridge. Beyond, in the dip between the hills, the wide stretch of the mire looked harmless, tawny coloured at this time of the year, with a glint of water here and there, and treacherously beautiful bright green patches to tempt the unwary.

She could hear men cursing and shouting directions to one another. Then she saw them on the edge of the mire, hiding her view of what was happening. She rode dangerously fast down the slope, her heart pounding as loudly as Bracken's hooves, hearing her own voice, high-pitched, begging, over and over, "Please God, please God, *please* . . ."
. . The mare tried to slow her pace but Jennifer was beyond reason now and ruthlessly kept her going. Then, suddenly, Bracken was down and Jennifer tossed over the pony's head. She lay where she had fallen, the breath knocked out of her.

Bracken scrambled up and made off towards the ridge. Jennifer heard renewed shouting from below. She got painfully to her knees and then to her feet. The little group of men had parted now and in the gap she could see the American thoroughbred, its chestnut colouring masked by a coating of slime, struggling to reach firm ground, with Darrell tugging at the reins. She could not see Alan.

She started down the slope, almost tripping over

her skirt. Gathering it into a bunch, she held it high, propriety, appearance, everything forgotten in her terrible urgency to reach Alan, to try and save him herself if no one else could.

Then she saw him, kneeling beside a stream. He had stripped off coat and shirt and was sluicing water over his head and shoulders. Jennifer stopped and closed her eyes as the world began to tip-tilt about her, so great was her relief. When she felt steadier, the murmured a fervent thanksgiving and went on down the slope.

Several of the men had gathered handfuls of bracken and were rubbing down the chestnut, while Darrell stood at its head. His breeches, like Alan's, were clogged with the foul-smelling ooze. Catching sight of her, he let go of the reins and moved towards her. She ignored him and went straight to Alan. As she spoke his name he glanced round, then rose to his feet. For a long moment they looked at one another. There was a sudden silence amongst the men. Then, regardless of spectators, of the fact that Alan was bare to the waist, Jennifer rushed forward and flung her arms around him.

He said, "Jenny, I'm filthy, and wet, and you'll get . . ."

"Do you think that matters? Do you think *any*-thing matters, except that you're alive? I was so frightened. Alan, hold me close, hold me *very* close."

He did not need asking twice. In a moment they

tions of the mire, hiding her view of what was hap-
for breath, while the watching men started to laugh,
then to cheer. When she turned to them, Jennifer
saw that Darrell was standing alone, head bowed,
hands hanging at his sides. All trace of arrogance
was gone now. He looked beaten and forlorn. Then
he straightened and came across to them.

"I must thank you, Mr Vicary, for saving my
horse at the risk of your own life. And I must also,
it seems, wish you and—and Jennifer . . ." His voice
trailed away, then with an obvious effort, he went
on. "I apologize for my conduct earlier this morning, Miss Haslam, and I would ask you to be generous enough to forget it. I should not like to think
that is how you will remember me, after I have
gone."

"Gone?" she repeated. "You—you are leaving?"

"Oh, yes. It is as you said, this is not where I
belong."

"You are returning to South Carolina?" she asked
in amazement.

He nodded. "I shall try to set matters right here
before I leave—for the commoners, and the tinners
to whom I promised employment."

"And Heronslea? What will happen to Heronslea?"

He shrugged. "I shall put it up for sale." Suddenly
he smiled. It was a rueful smile but it brought out
all she had found attractive in him. "Perhaps it

would be a good idea to let *you* interview prospective buyers, to make sure they are suitable."

"You do not bear me any malice, for . . . ?"

"Calling in Sir Robert Bratton? No, not any more. You had to do what you thought was right." He rubbed his hand down the cleanest part of his shirt, then took hold of hers. "I shall always remember you, and hope that things will go well with you —both," he added, turning to Alan.

"And I hope the same for you," she responded warmly. "*And* that you will soon find someone to —to fill the gap . . ."

But he had turned away. The last she saw of him, as she and Alan, arms entwined, went slowly up the slope, was as he breasted the ridge, leading the exhausted chestnut with the greatest care, on the first stage of his long journey home.